A LIFE *Worthwhile*

K.C. Swanson

A LIFE
Worthwhile

K.C. Swanson

Cover Design and Layout by Stacey Willey
Globe Printing, Inc., Ishpeming, Michigan
www.globeprinting.net

Published by
© Kevin Swanson

ISBN 978-1542985680

First Printing May 2017

This is a work of fiction. Names, characters, businesses, places, events and incidents are either the products of the author's imagination or used in a fictitious manner. Any resemblance to actual persons, or actual events is purely coincidental.

Chapter One

Prosperity had finally found Gage Gustafson. The twenty-three year old bachelor was quickly becoming accustomed to the urban life of Green Bay, Wisconsin. After returning to and graduating from Northern Michigan University, a fine school located in Michigan's Upper Peninsula, Gage quickly found work in Green Bay as a financial planner. Green Bay had been his home for only two weeks but he was already beginning to consider himself a successful young man.

Gage was born and raised in Ishpeming, a small town of 8,000 in the Upper Peninsula, known for its long history of logging and iron ore mining. As a member of a strong middle class family, Gage had enjoyed both the benefits provided by wonderful parents and the natural environment that surrounded him. Love for the outdoors was an innate natural characteristic of most men and women who were born in what was commonly called the U.P.

Gage was a very pleasant individual and most that knew of him held him in high regard. His quiet, modest and yet assertive personality prompted many to revolve around him as a dear friend and leader. Gage was a product of a strong and ambitious family and his demeanor mostly resembled that of his mother Sarah. Gage had worked hard to arrive at that particular moment in his life and he decided to reflect upon his journey to date, amidst a bustling group of entrepreneurs who walked the streets at noon on that fine day in September of 1996.

As Gage reached the street corner in downtown Green Bay with a cup of coffee in hand, a very familiar face passed him by. He knew her very well at one time as they dated for almost two years while attending college at NMU. Sherri Anderson walked by Gage without noticing him and he did not attempt to catch her attention. Through painful experience Gage had learned how a seemingly loyal and attractive woman could crush the hope of marriage, and the sight of Sherri brought him back in time.

Years before, during his first few semesters at Northern Michigan University, he was certain that true love was found in a blond haired, spirited young lady from Wisconsin. Her name was Sherri Anderson, and he was certain that he would make her his wife after graduation. Her robust personality was as attractive as her looks and her company was always exciting. But she had a way about her that forced Gage to be careless about other priorities; his grades were average at best, and relationships with friends and immediate family began to weaken. His mind became fogged by her ever present need for attention. Spare money, funded only by a part time job delivering beer, was solely dedicated to tending her every need.

It all ended on a cold Friday night in January when Gage unexpectedly showed up at a college sorority party to surprise Sherri. He was at his camp, a U.P term for cabin, with his cousin John for the weekend, but was not able to enjoy the time away because he did not want to be far from her side. Gage found Sherri in a corner at the party and she was not alone. Her big brown eyes were fixated on another man who was holding her close. Gage stopped in his tracks on a dime, his entire body shaking with immense shock and anger. He stood only twenty feet away, partially hidden by a dozen people who danced between Gage and his unfaithful queen. Gage watched as Sherri wrapped her arms around the tall stranger's neck as she approached his lips with her own. He turned away as they kissed and quickly headed for the door, bursting through anyone that stood in his path.

He reached his truck just as the tears could not be held back any longer. Choking and shaking, Gage opened and then quickly slammed the cab door shut, as he suddenly decided that driving away was not a good choice. Gage walked down the street at a brisk pace, trying to gather himself but not knowing what to do or where to go. His legs brought him to a bar around the corner where he drank two shots of whiskey and two beers. His mind was still reeling at what he had just witnessed, the pain was obvious in his eyes and it prompted the bar tender to ask if he was ok. Gage didn't answer and then quickly exited the bar when an attractive patron attempted to strike a conversation with him. The alcohol only intensified his agony as he trudged through the snow back to the sorority house to get his truck. As he neared the vehicle, Gage saw the pair again, this time standing on the porch in the midst of many others who were smoking and laughing as the stranger told a joke. Gage decided that he must approach them and his lips trembled even more as he caught the attention of Sherri Anderson. He wanted answers, and would not leave without them.

"Gage! What are you doing here?"

"How could you do this to me Sherri?" His speech was broken by the lack of oxygen flowing through his lungs.

He continued to approach slowly.

"I saw you Sherri. I saw you inside with this guy."

Sherri's embarrassment was apparent to all who stood on the porch as she frantically reached for the keys in her purse. She did not respond. The man she held closely inside looked surprised as well, it appeared that he was no stranger to Sherri Anderson.

"What's your problem?" he asked as he descended from the porch and moved slowly towards Gage, while discarding a cigarette.

Gage didn't hear him.

"I've put my heart and soul into this relationship Sherri, why are you doing this to me?" "Where the hell are my keys" she said, as if no one was speaking to her.

His pride was nearly nonexistent after pleading for answers

unsuccessfully, but Gage refused to allow her to leave him standing there with his integrity gone. As he turned to walk towards his truck he yelled angrily at Sherri one last time.

"Don't you ever come near me again! You're nothing more than a manipulative slut." Gage had never used a single derogatory word towards Sherri during the two years they had dated, but now he could not think of any that could hurt her enough. She began to cry like a victim as she ran back into the house with two friends at her side, and Gage then opened the door of his truck. As he lifted his right leg to step in, he felt a heavy hand crash down on his left shoulder. The stranger had a strong grip on Gage's jacket as he was spun around, forcing him to confront the other adversary.

"She's great in bed, just wanted you to know" said the man loudly so that his large audience of friends could hear him.

Gage could hear the laughter of the men nearby, he could see their faces under the dim glare provided by a street light above, which was suddenly mottled by heavy snowfall. The words directed at him from the foreigner tore his heart even more, further confirming that he was a fool in love with a temptress.

Gage was a scrapper no doubt; he had earned a reputation during high school that esteemed him as one of the best fighters in the area. He was strong but more importantly lightning fast, taught by his brother in their garage using a fifty pound punching bag. Roy Gustafson demonstrated to Gage how quickness and powerful jabs were the key ingredients of a successful scrap. When Gage was a sophomore in high school he observed his brother take on two pot heads in an alley behind the J.C. Penney store in downtown Ishpeming. Roy unleashed a furry of short left jabs followed by a jaw breaking right and soon there were two lads piled up against the brick wall of the store, looking like hell and spitting out blood. Their father, Robert Gustafson knew that fighting was a part of young men's lives but insisted that his boys only take part if there were no other options. He demanded that they not ever instigate a fight, nor breathe a word of fighting around their mother. Sarah Gustafson was a very peaceful and loving woman who never spoke a negative word about anyone; she did not appreciate the bag hanging in the garage and insisted that the boys not punch it in her presence.

"It's good exercise Ma" they would say when she asked why it was necessary to beat something so violently.

But their father would quietly encourage them to do so when their mother was not at home.

And so Gage now stood in front of a man who most definitely wanted to humiliate him even more by stripping what little pride remained. But the circumstances that surrounded this confrontation were vastly different than those during high school; Gage's spirit was already broken. He had no urge to fight, and instead turned away once again to get into the truck.

"I just want to get the hell out of here" Gage mumbled as he reached for the keys in the ignition.

"What a pussy" the man said, and then Gage felt a blow on his left cheek.

The open fisted back hand was a final attempt to draw Gage into battle with the confident stranger. The twenty degree temperature made it sting much more than it would have otherwise, and Gage brought his hand up to caress his cheek. He then turned to stare hard into the eyes of the stranger for the first time, the stranger that stole his girl.

Then it happened. The behavior of Gage changed from fear and hurtfulness to pure hatred, and he jumped out of the truck like an animal that had been cornered for much too long. His jacket was shed onto the road almost as quickly as the crowd encircled them. None of the fans were in favor of Gage, they were all shouting to his opponent.

"C'mon Pat, kick his ass. Hammer 'em."

The tall bastard heaved a round house punch that would have laid Gage out if it caught him, but he ducked it easily. Gage went in as his opponent reached back to cock another, and sprayed a quick left jab to Pat's right eye which sent him backwards five feet. The stranger expected it to be his turn but Gage surprised him with another painful left jab which was immediately followed by a well-placed, right handed freight train. The blow caught the left side of the enemy's nose with an eerie snap, and he immediately fell with both hands covering his face. Gage could see the steady stream of blood pouring onto the fresh white snow of the frozen street as Pat yelped in pain. Gage stood there for awhile hoping someone else would come at him before finally stepping into his truck. This time no one tried to stop Gage Gustafson.

He drove through the town of Marquette and back to his parent's home in Ishpeming. His mom greeted him at the door as always, and asked why he had come in from camp.

"I don't want to talk about it" he said as he walked by his concerned mother.

She immediately noticed the dried blood on his knuckles.

"Gage, what happened to your hand?"

Gage continued to walk towards his room.

"Just leave me alone mom."

The door slammed and Gage stayed in his room for the rest of the night. His mother didn't sleep that night after being notified by a close friend about the break up and fight that Gage had been involved in.

Chapter Two

Gage Gustafson, the young man of twenty-one years had most of his life ahead of him and yet he felt as though the world had come to an end. Sherri had called several times and had even sent him a letter, but he refused to return her calls and did not open the letter. He began to spend more time drinking with his non-academic friends than attending his classes at NMU, and his grades began to suffer. Months passed. He lost interest in his future and dropped out of college at the beginning of his junior year in September of 1994. Dreams of becoming a Wildlife Biologist for the Michigan Department of Natural Resources no longer appealed to him and his general outlook on life became sour. His family reached out to him on a daily basis, but Gage refused to admit to or discuss his problems. More than ever, his mom attempted to boost his confidence by complimenting him with tender care rather than criticizing him for dropping out of school. But his brother Roy, who was now married with children and who also owned a small logging business, began to grow impatient with Gage.

Roy found his brother at the Rainbow Bar on a Wednesday night in October after being called by his concerned mother.

"He's not been at work or home in two days Roy, your father has been to camp and he's not there either. Please find him Roy, I'm worried sick."

Gage was sitting at the bar in an obvious drunken stupor talking with his friend Dave who was in a similar condition.

Roy stepped up to the bar, said hello to the bartender and ordered himself a beer. Gage was so drunk that he didn't even notice his brother standing next to him until Roy spoke.

"Drunk again eh Gage, are you aware that mom and dad are worried sick about you?" Gage was surprised to see his brother at the bar.

"I didn't ask anyone to worry about me."

"That's what parents do; hopefully you'll be fortunate enough to be one someday."

"Tell them I don't need a baby sitter. I'll be home when I get there."

Roy was disgusted by the sight of his brother. Gage had not shaved in weeks, his hair was shaggy, and he was wearing dirty clothes under a torn Cardhart jacket. Roy was about to say something to portray his disgust when David stood up to intervene.

"How are you doing Roy?"

Roy was in no mood to make small talk.

"I'm fine Dave."

Roy kept his eyes on his brother who stared straight ahead.

"You know Roy, Gage is going through a tough time right now. He was really in love with that girl down at NMU. His plans were to marry her after school and have kids right away."

Roy finally turned to make eye contact with Dave.

"Yah I know, but it's time to move ahead, he's been moping around for months. He's allowing that skank to screw up his life."

Roy spoke loudly enough to ensure that Gage would hear, hoping that it might irritate his brother.

"Look at him, he dropped out of school and is only working part time delivering beer at the warehouse. He's drunk nearly every night and he looks like a bum."

Dave's eyes widened as if he were shocked by what Roy said.

"Isn't that a little harsh Roy? Gage and I are good buddies and we've been sticking together lately. I got laid off from the mill in Gwinn a few months ago so things aren't the greatest for me right now either. Maybe you should cut him some slack."

Dave continued on about how rough his own life had been. He had a poor upbringing, his mother and father both drank excessively and didn't set a good example for him or his sister. In Roy's opinion, Dave was doing a fine job of following their poor example.

Roy was tired. He had worked ten hours that day cutting timber by hand near the Peshekee Grade, then came home and cooked supper for his children before reading to them and tucking them in for the night. And now he was listening to a man who would rather complain about his problems than correct them, and impatience began to quickly set in.

"Dave, maybe you should move to Wisconsin, there's plenty of work down there." When Dave began to speak again Roy gently placed his hand across Dave's chest, and then removed him from his position between he and his brother. Roy stepped closer to Gage.

"I'm taking you home now" said Roy.

Gage glanced over and then ordered another beer and returned a look to his brother.

"Like fuck you will."

Roy was surprised by the words of his younger sibling but he knew that Gage had heard the scathing criticism in front of his friend and others. Roy realized he made a mistake in doing so, he should have waited until Gage was sober and approached him a bit more gently. He did not take kindly to criticism and was very much like his brother and father in that respect. Gage was drunk enough to boldly stare his brother in the eyes with a sarcastic scowl on his face. He had done this on only a few occasions in the past.

"Why don't you fuck off and leave me alone," Gage bellowed loudly, showing no fear whatsoever.

Roy Gustafson was not a person whom most would want to antagonize. At twenty-nine, Roy was eight years older than his brother, about the same height, and nearly twenty pounds heavier. Most of that twenty pounds consisted of muscle, constructed by working out with dumbbells and doing push-ups on a daily basis. And not just a few. Furthermore, Roy was in the best shape he'd ever been in simply because of his occupation. He was a contract logger that harvested timber for companies such as MeadWestvaco and International Paper, two of the largest landholders in the Upper Peninsula during the 1990's. Roy had purchased a very expensive piece of equipment called a skidder for which he hired one employee to operate. Roy cut the trees by hand using a Husqvarna chain saw and his operator would pick up the logs with the skidder and haul them back to the landing. Once enough wood was decked at the landing, a logging truck would pick it up and transport it to any number of mills in the U.P. or northern Wisconsin. The logging business was extremely dangerous and physically challenging, but could be very profitable if one put his heart into the job. Roy Gustafson put his heart into it every day, and he was becoming quite successful in doing so.

Roy had a very good reputation as a friend and father. He was very much a mild mannered individual and people were attracted to his kind and modest personality. Roy was a leader. He served as captain of the Ishpeming Hematite football team and received an "All State" award for his vicious record as a linebacker. Although he would have enjoyed the opportunity to play college football and had offers to take part, Roy had never been a good student in high school and decided to work in the woods instead. He was employed by another logger for three years who paid him well because he was so productive, but Roy then decided that more money could be made by working for himself. He had saved enough money in his first three years for a sizable down payment on a skidder, and the business took off from there.

Shortly after starting his business, Roy met a young woman named Kaylie Smith and she became pregnant a few months later. This was not planned but Roy knew that Kaylie was the one he had been seeking for quite some time. He asked her to marry him before the baby arrived and they bought a nice house in town on Michigan Street. Two years later, they had two beautiful children named Khora and Otto and appeared to be living the American dream. But Gage secretly despised Roy's wife, in his view she seemed to be quite lazy and non-appreciative. And worst of all, she didn't take much interest in her own children which troubled Gage very much.

Roy had allowed Gage to blow off some steam at the bar by rejecting his offer to take him home, but his temper began to flare after Gage became overly rude. He tried to contain himself one last time as he gently placed his hand on Gage's shoulder.

"Gage, mom is very worried about you, it's not fair to her for you to just disappear like this. You're an adult now, maybe you should start acting like one."

A sarcastic smile appeared on Gage's face, which was somewhat intimidating in combination with his bloodshot eyes and scruffy facial hair. He was about to let his feelings for Kaylie be known, after years of silent concern finally became disbanded from the alcohol.

"I wonder why you married Kaylie?" asked Gage in a curious and drunken tone.

"What?"

"Well, you have these great kids but besides that I don't see an upside."

"Careful Gage" responded Roy very seriously.

"You work your ass off. You come home and cook. You take care of the kids at night. What does she do Roy? She does nothing that's what."

"You better not say one more fuckin' thing about my wife Gage."

Many of the patrons in the Rainbow bar had become intrigued by the loud conversation.

David stood nearby with eyes wide open, totally surprised, and then pleaded quietly to his friend.

"Gage....Gage, we should leave now."

It was too late.

"Why don't you go home to that useless wife of yours" Gage yelled out as he stood up nose to nose with his brother.

Roy was shocked by the remarks, and Gage closely witnessed the mental pain inflicted by his comment transform into the vicious rage of a linebacker. Roy's teeth were clenched now and Gage figured he would knock them out rather than backing away. He approached with a right undercut that may have done the job if it were more accurately placed, but the alcohol had altered his perception of the target. The blow glanced off of Roy's left cheek, and then Gage came back with a left knowing full well that if he missed again the next punch would not be his own. Roy ducked the left hook and sprung back up within inches of Gage's face, grabbing his shirt collar and the hair beneath as he rose. Gage felt himself being lifted upward over the bar as Roy's knuckles painfully dug into his throat. He tried to break away but Roy's hands were much stronger than his. Roy had almost completely lost any remaining control, his testosterone pumped wildly as he drew back his right hand to finish it. Gage was still suspended by one arm when Roy came forward with an open handed blow to the top of his nose and eyes. Gage's head jolted back and he almost flipped over the bar but Roy held on tightly and pulled him back inward. Gage unknowingly settled back into the bar stool by his brother's hand, as blood streamed out of his nose and down his lips and chin. Everyone in the bar became very quiet, including Roy Gustafson. He looked around the bar, calmly apologized to the bartender for the commotion, and then walked his semi-conscious brother out the door with one hand on his belt.

Gage gathered himself to a certain extent after breathing the air from a cold night in March. He didn't resist his brother as Roy helped him get into the vehicle parked outside. Instead of bringing Gage home to his worried mother, Roy brought him to his own house, cleaned him up and then hauled him to the couch for the night.

"I love you Gage, I'm sorry that I hurt you."

Gage did not respond.

Roy picked up the phone and called his mother.

"He's alright mom, he'll sleep here tonight."

Roy didn't give his mom any of the details.

Roy sat quietly by himself for a long while, feeling quite badly about losing his temper on his brother. Like many others, Roy had faults and genetic imperfections that were difficult to overcome. He had been previously diagnosed with depression and kept this fact to himself despite feeling the urge to reach out to his mother, wife or brother. He struggled with the disease each and every day and relentlessly fought against it to the best of his ability. He researched the symptoms and fought them with fatherhood responsibilities, exercise and productiveness but eventually learned that he could not do it alone. He was losing the battle. He began to lose interest in hobbies once cherished such as fishing and hunting and could not understand why. No matter how well his occupation progressed, Roy was unsatisfied and it became a daunting challenge to emerge from bed each morning. But he disguised it well.

Depression and many associated suicides were all too familiar to many families in Michigan's Upper Peninsula. The winters were long and daylight hours short during those months, which intensifies the agony of many who suffer from various mental diseases. And despite the efforts of medical professionals and some compassionate community members, very few recognized depression as a disease. Instead, the foolish pride of many who suffered, paired with the inability of loved ones to reach out who had lost a family member to suicide, caused the disease to take many who should not have perished. Historically, the town of Ishpeming had been caught unprepared by a disproportionate number of suicide deaths. And the Gustafson family was affected more than most others, due to the prominence of mental illness in their family.

Roy's eldest cousin Kenneth took his life when Roy was just thirteen. The death of the twenty-two year old debilitated the entire family, who all loved Kenneth so dearly. Kenneth was a hero to Roy, he led the 1979 Ishpeming football team to a state championship as a small but terrifying linebacker and spent much time fishing and hunting with Roy. Kenneth was loved deeply by many, not because of his athleticism but because he was such a caring individual. He had severe depression and the internal pain intensified after graduating from high school. No one knew and he refused to seek help because he believed there was nothing anyone could do. The disease was disguised with a persuadable smile and even his own mother recognized no serious symptoms. But when the pain became too much to bear, Kenneth drowned himself in a stream after leaving a note apologizing to his family for what he was about to do. It is almost unimaginable that a person could take their own life knowing the endless grief and guilt their death will impose upon all who loved them, but this is the outcome of severe depression if help is not sought. Kenneth Gustafson simply could not see beyond his own agony, there was only one option that could stop the pain and that option was suicide. And he took it.

Eventually, and in part because of his cousin's death, Roy Gustafson convinced himself to see a doctor. He was feeling needlessly embarrassed as he waited in a room after speaking briefly with a nurse about his symptoms. Nervousness and pride overtook his demeanor as he heard a knock on the door.

"It's Dr. Pruett, may I come in?"

"Yes" answered Roy.

Dr. Lisa Pruett entered the room with a broad smile and a sense of friendliness that was apparent, but also somewhat reserved.

"I'm Dr. Pruett, it's a pleasure to meet you Roy."

"Likewise" responded Roy as he extended his hand to shake hers, even though he was not at all happy to be there.

The doctor seated herself next to Roy and examined his medical history on her lap. She was stunningly beautiful, with dark long hair streaming over a white overcoat and gorgeous blue eyes. She wore an attractive red dress and earrings that had a UP symbol engraved in each.

"How are you feeling Roy?"

Roy was hesitant, but also painfully aware that help was needed.

"Well......Well, I think I have some sort of clinical depression. And....And I just can't seem to overcome it on my own. I need your help doctor."

Roy looked defeated. Dr. Pruett smiled at him, attempting to remove the apprehension and embarrassment that he displayed.

"Roy, I want to first tell you that everything we discuss today is confidential, between you and me. We can help you get through this."

"Good" answered Roy with a phony smile.

"But I need you to be completely honest with me so that we can clearly understand your symptoms, deal?"

"Deal."

"Good. So tell me Roy, have you lost interest in some of the things you typically enjoy?"

Roy sat forward in his chair, brought his hands together while placing his elbows on his knees, and looked downward at the floor. There was a long pause as Roy attempted to put his feelings into words for the first time.

"It's ok Roy, take your time."

"Yes."

Dr. Pruett waited patiently for him to continue.

"Yes I have. I've lost interest in hunting and fishing, and it seems I have lost the urge to be around other people altogether, other than my own children."

"I don't enjoy hobbies as I once did, and I wish I could just stay in bed on most days, especially during the winter."

Dr. Pruett sat back in her chair, crossed her legs and brought a closed hand to her chin.

"So you would like to stay in bed on most days because you

are sad, or because you are tired, or both?"

"Fatigue consumes me, and I think the fatigue is caused by sadness. My job requires a lot of physical labor that causes me to become tired but this is different. This is sadness.... hopelessness."

"And what do you feel sad or hopeless about?" asked Pruett.

"Pretty much everything except my children and sometimes, sometimes I feel hopeless even about them. They bring me joy and some energy, but it's a constant battle to feel any sense of happiness."

"I see."

Roy continued to open up.

"But here's what I don't understand, there is no reason for me to feel this way. I have everything a man could ask for; a beautiful family, great friends and a thriving business and yet I feel hopeless. I have some issues in my marriage but I doubt many are perfect, I have much to be thankful for and yet I'm not satisfied, never content."

"How long have you been feeling this way Roy?"

"Since after high school and it seems to be getting worse as I get older. But I hide it well, no one knows, not even my wife. I work hard every day and have built a very successful company, and yet it's not enough. I thought more money would help but it doesn't."

Dr. Pruett wanted Roy to continue talking so that she could accurately assess the severity of his illness.

"Money certainly doesn't buy happiness, not for long anyway" she said.

"I try every day to overcome these feelings by being a good father, by being ambitious, by exercising, by praying, but I just can't seem to beat it."

The room became silent again. Roy looked as though he were about to break down.

"Well Roy, I have good news for you."

"What would that be?" he asked.

"You have taken a big step, perhaps the most difficult part of beating this illness, by coming here today. You have finally realized that you can't do this on your own Roy."

"Now listen to me carefully" she continued.

Roy raised his head to make eye contact with her while containing the same posture, the pain in his eyes obvious. Dr. Pruett scooted her chair closer to Roy.

"There's not a doubt in my mind that you have depression Roy. But the good news is that this is usually, almost always, a treatable disease. It is also a very common illness; approximately ten percent of the US population has some form of depression or other mental illness."

"Do I need medication?"

"Absolutely, but please know there is nothing to be ashamed of Roy. Your illness is caused by a chemical imbalance in your brain, which cannot be overcome without medication. We will try an anti-depressant at a low dosage initially, and then adapt from there based on your progress. We will meet every few months or definitely more often if you feel the need."

"Ok" said Roy.

"Your honesty is appreciated Roy, it's the only way we can assess this. I know it's hard for you to talk about this, but you are doing so very well today."

"Thank you" Roy replied with a genuine smile.

"I already feel better after talking with you."

"I have a few more questions Roy."

"Yes?"

"Have you ever contemplated suicide, ever think about taking your own life?"

Roy's smile changed to an expression of seriousness.

"No....No I would never do that to my family."

"Do you have any history of mental illness in your family?"

Roy paused for a moment again.

"Yes. My cousin, whom I was very close to, he killed himself long ago. He was my idol."

"I'm very sorry. You assume he had depression?"

"There's no other explanation, he had a great life, he was a pleasant person and he was a great athlete. My uncle also committed suicide, he hung himself."

Dr. Pruett jotted down a few notes and then turned again to Roy with another broad smile.

"We're going to make you better Roy."

"Wonderful, thank you so much Dr. Pruett."

As Roy exited the doctor's office at Bell Hospital his hopelessness continued to be replaced by optimism. He felt markedly better after speaking with Dr. Pruett, better than he had in a very long time, fully believing brighter days were coming. As he drove to a nearby pharmacy to pick up the anti-depressant prescription, he felt a bit guilty for not being entirely truthful with Dr. Pruett. Roy had indeed considered taking his own life on more than one occasion, when the internal pain seemed too much to bare, but once again he convinced himself that he would not have done it.

"Never" he said to himself out loud.

Chapter Three

The next morning Gage woke up early with a pounding headache and throbbing nose. He stumbled to the bathroom to face himself in the mirror. It was a gruesome sight, his nose was swelled and two shiners were beginning to form around his eyes. He resembled Rocky Balboa after a championship fight, except his fight only lasted about ten seconds and he was not the victor. Gage quietly snuck out of the house without waking Kaylie and the children, and began the three block trek to his parents' home. He noticed that Roy's truck was gone, he had already left for work. It was 6:00 a.m. The walk home was agonizing for a beaten and hung over young man, but it did him some good. He felt terrible for saying what he had about Roy's wife, so terrible in fact that he believed the swat from his brother was almost justifiable. Almost. It would have been much worse had Roy struck him with a closed fist, Gage would have been unconscious for a long while.

Gage crept in the door like a burglar so as not to wake his mom, but he heard her get out of bed as soon as his foot touched the carpet. He pulled his cap down low to hide his ridiculous face and walked straight towards his bedroom.

"Gage, where the hell have you been the last two days?"

He hadn't heard that tone from his mother in a very long time and realized that he had finally pushed her too far. He stared at the floor, his mother had blocked the entrance to his room and this time she was demanding answers.

"Look at me when I'm speaking to you."

Gage raised his head, fully expecting her to break down and cry at the sight of her wounded son. He was certain that her fantastic nurturing abilities would overcome any anger she felt for him. He wouldn't pay attention as she filled him with compliments, telling him that he's a wonderful young man with a prosperous life just ahead. He would milk every bit of attention she offered after he mentioned Sherri Anderson's name, and then borrow some money for the next night's visit to the bar. But as Gage's eyes met those of his mother, he immediately noticed that they looked even more deadly than his brother's the night before.

"What have you been doing?" she screamed. "I'm fed up with your bullshit Gage."

This was not the reaction he had hoped for, it seemed his mother was about to go on a rampage. There was no sympathy in her body language as she screamed on and on about how he was letting his family down. When Gage thought it was just about over his father emerged from the bedroom, wearing long johns inside out and rubbing the sleep from his eyes. He stood behind his wife with a most concerned look on his face, seemingly as surprised by her demeanor as Gage was.

"I'll handle this Sarah. Gage, there's a right road and a wrong road through life and you're headed……"

"SHUT UP ROBERT! I'm not through with him."

Robert looked at his normally soft-spoken wife with shock as she scolded him further for interrupting her. When he saw the redness in her face he turned around and walked straight back into his bedroom.

"Mom I'm sorry. I've just been going through a rough time lately."

Gage waited for her to soften up a bit.

"I'm going to get back on track now Mom."

"You're damn right you are, I want you out of my house within a week."

As she walked out of the room, Sarah Gustafson threw four

pamphlets in front of Gage on a table. Gage was stupefied by his mother's anger; he picked up the pamphlets and walked into his room. Each of the pamphlets had a title; Army, Navy, Air Force, and Marines.

And so Gage Gustafson found himself at a pivotal point in his life. He was shocked by his mother's new personality, she was obviously deeply disappointed in her son for the way he had carried on over the past several months. Gage would no longer be a freeloader at his parents' house, they would not continue to financially support him. He was very depressed as he flipped through the military pamphlets in his room, unable to imagine himself as a soldier. He stayed in his room all day while taking brief naps that were consistently interrupted by overwhelming feelings of guilt and despair.

His mother was feeling a different kind of pain. She desperately wanted to reach out to Gage but would not allow herself to make the same mistake once again. Telling herself repeatedly that this was a primary example of "tough love," she kept her distance from her son and did not cook supper for him that evening. Gage Gustafson was at rock bottom; his life could either continue to spiral out of control beyond the possibility of regaining his integrity, or a decision would be made to move forward. He decided to move from his house as soon as possible but he would first need to find an apartment and a full time job to pay for rent.

Later that evening Gage walked back to the Rainbow Bar to retrieve his truck. He was relieved it had not been towed away and was brushing off an inch of snow when Dave arrived, also on foot.

"Holy shit Gage, you look awful!"

"Thanks Dave."

"Your brother is one tough fucker, he lifted you up over the bar with one arm and..."

"Stop Dave. I'm aware of what he did."

"You shouldn't have bad mouthed his wife like that Gage, you really pissed him off."

"No shit Dave."

"Did you really mean all those things you said about her?"

Gage knew he could confide in his long-time friend.

"Yes...Yes but I shouldn't have said it in front of you and others at the bar."

"You're right Gage, you shouldn't have done it when you were drunk either."

"You are really not helping me David."

Dave realized that Gage was not appreciative of his advice and decided to change the subject.

"Well what's done is done, how about a beer on me Gage?" said Dave as he gestured towards the entrance of the Rainbow bar.

Gage pondered the appealing invitation for a few moments.

"No Dave. I'm done with this drinking bullshit for a while."

"So I'll see you tomorrow night then?"

"Nope" responded Gage as he stepped into his truck.

"I'll call you in a week or so Dave, I need to straighten myself out and I suggest you do the same."

"O.K." said Dave sarcastically as he walked into the bar.

With two black eyes and what was left of his pride hanging from his sleeve, Gage showed up at the door step of Tasson Distributing Company on Monday morning. Tasson Distributing was located on Lake Shore Drive in Ishpeming, a multi-million dollar business overlooking a portion of Lake Bancroft. Gage had worked at the warehouse part time since he graduated from high school. The extra money helped him to make payments on his truck and also provided him with a limited amount of cash for entertainment. But it was his parents who financed the vast majority of his college expenses and provided room and board in their home. Things were different now. All of his future decisions would be financially supported by him alone and he was attempting to make the first big step. He expected Mike Tasson, the owner of the business, to be angry about not showing up for work at all the week prior, and Gage could sense a bit of resentment in Mike's expression as he approached. Gage was nervous.

"Hi Mike. I'm sorry I didn't show up to help out last week, it was a big screw up."

"You look like hell."

"I know."

"Heard your brother had to kick your ass."

"That's debatable. He's lucky I was drunk, it wouldn't have been so easy otherwise."

Mike smiled.

"Well Gage, you're only a part time employee but I still expect you to show up for work. It's not characteristic of you to skip work like that."

Gage was relieved that Mike hadn't been more upset then he was.

"Your dad told me about what's going on with you Gage, are you really going to behave this way because of one young lady?"

Ishpeming was a small town, everyone knew everyone's business.

"I am not going back to school, so I thought I'd ask for a full time job instead."

Mike looked Gage over before replying.

"I just put an ad in the paper for a full time guy, but I need to depend on that person to show up and work hard every day."

Gage had earned a great reputation at Tasson's prior to not showing up the week before. He had obtained a Commercial Driver's License and became known by the owners and employees as a "work horse". Gage had on many occasions left the warehouse at 7:00 a.m. with 500 cases and 20 kegs of beer and returned with an empty truck by 2:00 p.m. The average deliveryman at Tasson Distributing was about half as efficient as Gage Gustafson.

"Well then I'm your man" said Gage with very pronounced black eyes and a smirk on his face.

Mike returned the smile and instructed Gage to return the

following morning to begin his full time job.

His hourly wage would be $8.00 per hour, in addition to health insurance and a 401(k). "Don't fuck this up Gage" added Mike sternly as he turned and walked away.

A notion of excitement overtook Gage for the first time since before finding Sherri Anderson with another man. He now considered himself to be free of college obligations, and would be able to live his life as he would so choose. He found a decent apartment downtown for $300 a month with utilities included. Gage was not satisfied with the hourly wage offered but also knew that any number of men would accept it if he hadn't, it was a fair start.

Good jobs of any kind, other than the health care industry, were extremely hard to find in the Upper Peninsula, where the average annual income of single wage earner was about $20,000 per year. The somewhat depressed economy was fueled mostly by logging, mining, and tourism but was also aided by a handful of colleges and hospitals. Cleveland Cliffs, a large iron ore mining company based in Cleveland, Ohio, was the largest employer in the Ishpeming area. The men and women that worked for Cleveland Cliffs were paid very well, but most were required to take part in grueling shift work. It was a well-known fact that swing shifts were very hard on the mind, body, and schedules demanded by family life. But to most this was a much more appealing alternative than leaving the beautiful Upper Peninsula in order to find work elsewhere.

Gage arrived at home that night to a mother who was a bit friendlier than the last time he had spoken to her. Supper was served to a relatively quiet table at 5:00 p.m., but abrupt conversation began when Gage revealed to his parents that he now had a full time job. His mom and dad were very happy to hear that he had finally taken a step forward and many questions were asked, and answers given about the job and his new apartment. Gage went to his room after supper and decided to begin packing his belongings. There was no hurry to do so, he couldn't move into the apartment until the following Monday and all of his possessions would fit into two medium sized boxes. It would not be a large undertaking to get himself moved.

Gage showed up for work fifteen minutes early the next morning and waited for the doors to open. He had stopped at a nearby gas station to buy a can of snuff before arriving, it was decided the night before that he would pick up a new habit to replace the one that was slowly leading to his demise. At least for awhile anyway.

"Hello Gage, welcome back" yelled out Tommy Stevens as he opened the business for the day.

Tommy was the warehouse manager and he also delivered beer when necessary. Gage had always admired Tommy's work ethic and from day one, this was part of the reason that he himself worked so hard. All of the employees were quite encouraged by the return of Gage Gustafson. They all enjoyed his company but were more interested in his return because their work load would now lessen somewhat. Gage walked into the warehouse with an apprehensive smile on his face, surrounded by thousands of cases of beer produced by companies such as Miller, Coors, and Heileman. The Tassons' had a business that would flourish under any circumstance. Most people who resided in the area drank beer when they were happy or sad, heartbroken or in love, employed or on unemployment.

The salespersons and deliverymen of the company were charged with the responsibility of marketing the product and delivering it with a friendly smile. All of the trucks were loaded the night before so Gage hopped into the one he was instructed to drive and headed for each and every bar in Ishpeming and the nearby town of Negaunee. One by one each of the drivers returned to the warehouse in order of the most ambitious to the most average. All of the trucks were loaded for the next day's routes before the business was closed at 4:30 p.m. Gage was tired after supper that night, he lay on the couch and watched TV for an hour before deciding to drive to his brother's house. The two shiners that his brother inflicted upon him were beginning to slowly fade, but the guilt that he felt about the comment made regarding Roy's wife had not. Greeted at the door by his nephew and niece, he hugged them and apologized for not coming to see them for quite some time. Roy looked over his brother from his lazy boy as Gage sat down on the couch.

"You're looking better Gage, mom told me that you got in full-time down at the warehouse."

Gage did look better despite his bruised eyes. He had paid a sorely needed visit to the barber, his face was cleanly shaven and he was wearing a decent set of clothes rather than the usual Cardhart outfit with black Iceman boots.

"Where's Kaylie?" Gage asked as he hugged and kissed Khora and Otto while they sat on his lap.

"She's out with that worthless Barbara again."

Gage didn't need to ask. He knew Barbara Johnson was bad news through and through. She was also married with children but spent more time in the bars with other men than she did with her own kids. Barbara and Kaylie had been friends for a long time. Roy had attempted to break up the friendship by pleading with his wife on a number of occasions but it had never worked. Rumors of Barbara's infidelity reached nearly every home in the town of the people that knew her, except her own. She was an attractive woman who wouldn't allow her high school popularity to diminish even after she married and had children. She frequented bars often, to as she claimed, relieve the stress of raising kids. Her stress relief was much different than most mothers in that she had affairs with many single and married men, but managed to somehow keep it from her hard working husband. Barbara Johnson was popular alright, but she was not the type that a man would want his wife to be associated with.

After playing a few games of Buzz Lightyear Yahtzee with Khora and Otto while refereeing battles between them, Gage returned to the couch. The two brothers quietly sat together watching a special about Saddam Hussein while the kids watched a movie in the play room. Gage was trying to build up the courage to apologize to his brother but it took much longer than he imagined, because he truly believed that Kaylie was not worth his while.

"Roy I apologize for what I said about Kaylie. I was drunk and way out of line. I hope you can forgive me for that."

Roy continued to watch T.V. until the next commercial, purposely causing his brother to feel even more uncomfortable.

"Kaylie didn't have a proper childhood like us Gage. She's been off drugs for almost a year now and has been trying to find a decent job that she would enjoy."

Gage sensed that his brother had at least partially forgiven him and decided that time would heal the rest, and so they sat together awhile longer before Gage said goodnight.

During the drive back to his parent's house, Gage thought about his sister in-law. Kaylie knew that Gage was not very fond of her and she made a point to explain her misgivings to him a few years after her marriage to Roy. Her father had died of alcoholism when she was six years old and she was taken from her mother at the age of eight. She was removed from her mother's custody because of drug abuse and neglect, and her mom died from an overdose about a year later. Kaylie bounced from one foster home to the next while attending school in Ishpeming. Like her mother, Kaylie embraced alcohol and drugs at a very young age and finally dropped out of school during her senior year.

At that time Roy had been out of school for a couple of years, working hard in the woods as a logger. Roy was very popular during high school and afterwards but he did not have the looks to demand the love of a beautiful woman. Kaylie was somewhat rough looking but quite gorgeous as well, and Roy showed a great deal of interest in her when they met at a party near Deer Lake. Roy was a shy fellow but he built up the courage to approach her after their eyes met across the fire. They hit it off and started to date immediately. Roy was politely warned by several people, including his brother, that Kaylie was not worthy of him but he took it upon himself to make it work. Roy fell in love partially because she needed a good man so desperately. Kaylie was honest with him about her past and made a solemn promise to Roy that she would become a woman that he deserved. His cautious demeanor was thrown aside as he dove into a very serious relationship. Most of the people who surrounded the life of Roy Gustafson were worried about his reckless love for Kaylie, but she sensed everyone's apprehension and began to put forth the effort to eliminate it. While working as a waitress at Buck's restaurant she enrolled in evening classes to obtain her GED and graduated a few months later. Roy rewarded her with a proposal to marry him as they overlooked the waterfall of the Black River, located near the Gustafson camp. She eagerly accepted and then informed him of a positive pregnancy test that was taken just hours before. The timing was perfect, and Roy had never been happier. His love for Kaylie had lessened the fatigue and sadness of the mental disease that plagued him.

The news of the baby and Roy's proposal was perceived to be very much premature by his family. But Roy's mother Sarah convinced herself that it was meant to be and requested that Gage and his father not ever speak negatively about Kaylie again. Kaylie was beginning to prove that Roy deserved her as much as she deserved him. But she had a long way to go and Gage was the most skeptical of any. He wanted to approach his brother before the wedding to convey his worries about Kaylie, but wasn't able to build up the nerve. Gage was also concerned that if he did say something to Roy it would not be taken well and would ultimately lead to the demise of their close relationship.

And so the ceremony took place six months after Roy proposed. By now Kaylie was looking very much like a pregnant mother to be and she and Roy had finally found a nice home on Michigan Street. The house was totally in order for the arrival of their first born, a fabulous daughter named Khora.

Kaylie had behaved like an honorable wife for nine months,

but after the baby was born Roy quickly noticed the onset of irrational behavior. Kaylie's interest in the baby was typical of any mother at first, but she then began to become despondent and aggravated. Roy relieved as much pressure as he was able to by supporting Kaylie's decision to work no longer, and by taking care of Khora each night after returning home from his job. Over a period of time, Kaylie departed almost as quickly as he arrived to enjoy a few hours of freedom with her friends over coffee. Roy understood that it was hard for Kaylie to stay at home all day with a newborn and he enjoyed every second spent with his well-behaved daughter during the evening, but it started to bother him after some months of Kaylie's escapes to the coffee shop. The challenges faced by the marriage intensified when Roy's logging business began to expand. His exciting obligation demanded more of his time in order for it to be a success. Roy would not allow things to play out otherwise. He was very optimistic that he could be an outstanding father, provider, and husband, but he would need some cooperation from his wife. The wages that Roy earned for his efforts as a dedicated business owner definitely helped to ease the burden of a young mother, and Kaylie's outlook started to improve as she purchased many nice things for herself and the baby. She had never dreamed she would live this good.

A baby boy named Otto was born two years later and Roy Gustafson was certain that his life could not be any more perfect. But after some time Kaylie had become mysteriously unsatisfied once again. Her coffee shop outings in the evenings transformed into pool league, dart league, and other activities that would get her out of the house. Roy continued to tolerate her absence because she had convinced him that she would go crazy without it, but he started to worry that she was reverting to her old state of mind. After all, Roy was acquainted with many other women that did not feel the need to abandon their husbands and children during most nights. When Kaylie was home, Roy treated her like a queen and gracefully fulfilled all parenting responsibilities while she did absolutely nothing. Gage noticed this and began to secretly despise Kaylie for treating her husband and children as a tiring obligation rather than a family that loved her so dearly.

Gage stepped up like his brother and became a dedicated uncle to the point where Khora and Otto would be noticeably upset with him if he didn't visit at least three times over the course of any given week. Gage made time to spend with the kids throughout his entire relationship with Sherri Anderson. But after they broke up he didn't have the urge to visit them very often, and he heard about it that night before apologizing to his brother.

Chapter Four

Gage moved out of his parent's home after work on the following Monday. He had earned enough money during his first week of work to purchase a second hand couch, kitchen table, and television. His mom and dad had given him his bedroom set, a recliner, and a few end tables that would complete the look of the apartment. When he returned to his parents to clean his bedroom later that evening his mom hugged him for a long time. It was obvious that she was fighting back tears as she spoke to him.

"I love you very much Gage. Your father and I want the best for you and we felt that you weren't applying yourself."

Gage gently touched his mother's cheeks with his hands and gave her a big smile.

"Mom, you gave me just what I needed, a good kick in the ass. Now don't be sad, I'll be over to visit you and dad often."

Gage's first night in the apartment was very satisfying. He felt much like a responsible person now as he looked out his window onto Main Street in downtown Ishpeming. The apartment looked like that of a bachelor with little taste; it was lacking the touch of sensitivity normally provided by a wife or a mother. But at this stage of his life, Gage was quite happy with the layout of the apartment and the independence it symbolized. As he sat in his recliner glancing over the latest issue of *U.P. Real Estate* magazine, Gage wondered if he would someday be able to capture his dream of buying property. He then took a few minutes to reflect on the previous year of his life, which by far was the most challenging period he had faced so far. After dropping out of school at the beginning of his junior year, Gage had fallen from grace in a way that he thought not possible. He decided that he would never again allow himself to be brought down to such a level. An attractive young woman had nearly led to his demise, but Gage was now certain that he was over Sherri Anderson. He had learned that when faced by a challenge, if he didn't rise and conquer it, it would conquer him, and he was determined never to let that happen again.

Gage reported to work the next morning feeling optimistic. He enjoyed the job in general and took pride in the fact that his daily contribution would lead in part to a more successful business, for which he could eventually receive a promotion to a salesman position. Even though he enjoyed the hard work associated with loading and delivery, Gage knew that he may not be mentally challenged enough to work at it for the rest of his career. And so he set a goal to become a salesman within one year of employment. Such a position would utilize some of the skills and knowledge learned in college as his minor was in business. While tending his route that Monday morning in early April of 1995, he entertained the familiar idea of someday owning his own business after running into his godmother in town.

"Hello Gage" said Lillian Gauthier as she opened the trunk of her car.

"Well hello there" responded Gage as she approached him with the usual hug.

Lillian Gauthier was a retired Ishpeming school teacher and successful business owner, well known in the community as a pillar of achievement and mentorship. She took particular interest in her godson and as usual did not waste the opportunity to advance his thought process.

"I hear you've had some troubles and I'm glad you're pulling through it Gage."

"Yep."

"What's next, when do you plan to return to college if at all?"

"I'm not planning to go back, I have a good job delivering beer and my goal is to become a salesman within a year or two."

"That's wonderful Gage. If that career is suitable you could have a great life here in Ishpeming."

"That's my plan."

"But do yourself a favor Gage, don't make any hasty decisions right now. You're a young man with much potential and likely many ideas are running through your head."

Gage listened carefully.

"Give yourself some time to figure things out. Maybe you'll return to college and maybe you won't, maybe you'll be a wildlife biologist and maybe you won't, just don't sell yourself short Gage."

"O.K."

"Do you remember telling me long ago that your dream was to own a business someday?"

"Yah I remember."

"Well that prospect might pop back into your mind any day, enjoy those ideas and don't rush through them."

Gage thanked Lillian as she kissed him on the cheek, and then she quickly moved along with her ambitious day.

For the first time since November of 1994 the temperature exceeded forty-five degrees. A brutal winter that punished Marquette County residents with several feet of snow and consistent below average temperatures was finally over. Many of the retired fled from the U.P. early in the winter to take up a temporary residence in places such as Florida or Arizona, where they would enjoy good food and skin tanning weather. Those that did not prefer or could not afford to travel south would spend most of their time in-doors, only to expose themselves to the wicked elements while walking behind a snow blower after a storm. But most working class adults enjoyed U.P. winters for a variety of reasons. Many outdoor enthusiasts took part in such hobbies as cross country and downhill skiing, ice fishing, rabbit hunting, trapping, snow shoeing, and snowmobiling. Snowmobiling in particular was considered to be a temporary backbone of the U.P. economy. Numerous trails were maintained throughout the Peninsula which lured thousands of tourists during winter months. Tourists bolstered the profits of numerous hotels and other businesses which sustained them throughout the winter. But only an occasional snowmobile could be heard on that day in early April as the snow rapidly melted away.

Gage finished his route that day at the Rainbow bar, he had last been there on the night that his brother quickly overtook him in front of a number of people. Even though his black eyes were faded, Gage was a bit embarrassed as he strolled in with a hand cart mounted with six cases of beer. He was greeted by the owner and a few customers that never seemed to be elsewhere as he unloaded his cart, and then returned to the truck for two kegs of Miller Lite. As he placed the kegs in the coolers behind the counter his good friend Dave walked into the bar with two other friends.

"Hello Gage, how do you like your new apartment?"

"I like it just fine" Gage said as he shook hands with the three men.

They talked about the usual things while Gage waited for payment from the owner of the bar. Dave explained that his unemployment checks were soon to run out.

"I'm gonna have to find another job real soon."

Gage was fully aware that Dave possessed the skills necessary to carry out a number of different occupations but he also knew that Dave lacked initiative. He was the type that would live off of unemployment for his entire life if the system allowed. But Gage had a special place in his heart for Dave because they had grown up together, grown up together under entirely different circumstances.

During his drive back to the warehouse, Gage wondered why

so many people were satisfied with being less than average. He himself had a long way to go before others would consider him to be a productive individual; after all, Gage spent much of the last year doing not much at all. But he was back on track now, a much stronger person with a renewed positive outlook on life.

Chapter Five

Gage arrived at his apartment that night to a familiar and pleasing aroma. His mother had prepared her famous meatballs and spaghetti sauce and left it simmering on the stove. She had stocked his refrigerator and shelves with healthy foods and vegetables. A note was left on his kitchen table with her signature smiley face, apologizing for barging into the apartment while he was gone and instructing him to eat all of his food groups every day. He ate two helpings of spaghetti before driving to his parents' home to thank them for supper and the weeks' supply of groceries. He stayed there for awhile and discussed the upcoming opener of brook trout season with his father and then drove to his brother's house for a brief visit.

The 1890's Victorian home had been recently re-roofed and re-sided and the hardwood floors reclaimed, making it one of the most beautiful homes in Ishpeming. Khora and Otto were excited to see him as usual, but their mother was in one of her moods and barely welcomed Gage as he walked in the door.

"Hello Gage" she mumbled without so much as glancing up from the television.

"Hi Kaylie. Where's Roy?"

"He's working late, he called and said a hose blew on the skidder and he needs to replace it right away. Now I have to miss my bowling league tonight and the kids are driving me crazy."

Gage had heard it all before. She had also dropped a hint to Gage, hoping that he would offer to watch the kids so that she could join her useless friends for a night of drinking, bowling, and God only knows what else.

"I'll stay until Roy gets home Kaylie."

"Really, are you sure Gage?"

"Yah, it's no problem, I was planning to stay for awhile anyway."

Kaylie was immediately energized as she removed herself from the couch and bolted for her room to change clothes and freshen up. She emerged ten minutes later with her usual "night out" clothes on that consisted of tight jeans and a short cut shirt. Kaylie Gustafson was a rough but very attractive woman.

"Roy should be home at around 9:00 p.m." she said as she walked by her kids and Gage, failing to thank him or say goodbye to the children. The door shut and Gage looked down upon his niece and nephew with a sense of relief.

The kids were sitting on their uncle's lap listening to the sixth book of the evening when their father opened the door.

"Hi guys. How bout' a hug."

Roy dropped to his knees as Khora and Otto sprung into his arms and he kissed them both before asking Gage where his wife was.

"She's at bowling league, I offered to stay and watch the kids until you got home."

"I should have known she wouldn't miss an opportunity to go out with her friends" said Roy. "Thanks for watching the kids, they sure like it when you visit."

Gage stayed for another hour after Roy tucked the kids into bed and they talked about a variety of topics including Roy's business. Gage looked up to his brother and listened carefully after inquiring about his progress as an entrepreneur. Roy explained that he had been involved in numerous real estate transactions where he bought land and then sold it for a profit after holding it for a relatively short period of time. He continued to do this until he could afford to pay cash for a nice piece of forested property that he would manage for timber and retain for his family. Roy had accumulated almost one full section, equivalent to 640 acres, of forested land over a five year period. Gage was baffled by his ongoing success.

"My God Roy, that's wonderful!"

Roy continued to explain how he planned to acquire more land by sustainably cutting some of what he had and would use the profits to purchase more.

"There's a lot of money in wood Gage and God isn't making any more land."

Even though Roy's expertise in the forestry business was harvesting wood, he had learned a great deal about proper timber management from industrial foresters and from various books that he read at night. Roy had indeed become a successful businessman and entrepreneur. Most were not aware, but his assets were already worth more than one million dollars.

Before Gage left that evening, Roy told him a very interesting story about a 320 acre parcel that he had purchased a few days before from a couple of drug addicts from Florida. While traveling to his work site, Roy stopped at a gas station for a cup of coffee where he overheard two men talking to the store clerk about land they wished to sell. Roy ascertained that they were not from the area because of their tan and slight accent, and he decided to approach them outside of the store to inquire about the land. They eagerly explained to Roy that they had inherited 320 acres from their grandfather who had recently passed away, and that they had no interest in holding it. The men were from Florida, they were driving an older model two-wheel drive car and made it obvious that they wanted to sell the land quickly and then return to Florida. They handed Roy a map of where the property was located and asked if he might be able to give them directions. After looking over the map briefly, Roy knew where the property was and decided to bring them to it himself. The small convoy drove west through the small towns of Humboldt, Champion, and Michigamme, and then turned south on the Imperial Heights Road. They reached the Fence River Grade and continued south to an area near the Cut Across Road where Roy pulled over. Roy knew the area quite well. He and Gage had hunted for ruffed grouse, also known as partridge by local residents, and fished for brook trout near the Fence Grade on numerous occasions.

Roy tried to contain his excitement as they walked through the parcel. The men from Florida were busy swatting and cussing at mosquitoes that seemed to greatly enjoy the taste of foreign blood while Roy examined the gorgeous timber that consisted of sugar maple, yellow birch, and a few conifers. Roy was amazed, by his estimation the land had not been cut in at least seventy years and it was the finest stand of timber that he had ever laid his eyes on. The hardwood stood very tall and straight and many of the trees had a diameter of at least twenty inches. By rough calculation, he determined that there were approximately forty-five cords of pulp and 5,000 board feet of lumber per acre. He had to do the calculation three times in order to convince himself that the volume estimate was correct.

With compass and map in hand, Roy led the men over several hardwood ridges before stopping at the edge of a small cedar swamp near the northwest corner of the property, knowing full well that the mosquitoes would be in great numbers near the swamp. He found a fresh pile of bear scat and pointed it out to the southerners.

"Bear? What kind of bear? Grizzlies?" asked Frank Richards, the eldest of the two brothers.

His younger brother Brett looked at Roy wide-eyed, waiting for an answer. Roy looked around as if he were concerned for their safety.

"Black bear. There are plenty of them in this area. There not as big as Grizzlies but they're every bit as ferocious."

The men looked at each other, hoping that one would console the other but instead they exchanged glances of fear. Roy watched a mosquito land on Frank's ear that was equivalent in size to a small humming bird. Frank shrieked with obscenities as the fly drove its needle like stinger into his flesh.

"These flies are eating us alive, we should get back to the Hotel" Frank said as he frantically swatted at the swamp beasts.

"Are you interested in buying the land?"

Roy did not want to express his entire interest in the land, but he knew if a realtor became involved the price would increase substantially and be much more than he could afford.

"How much do you want for it?"

"Well, we were told by some people in town that we should be able to get $800 per acre, but we're in a hurry to get back to Florida so we would accept a little less."

Frank looked to Roy for a response after nothing was said for a few moments.

"$800 per acre is way out of my range."

Roy was certain the land was worth more than $800 per acre because of the tremendous timber value found in the veneer logs, but he simply could not afford that amount.

"How much can you offer? We need the cash so we won't accept a land contract. Why don't you think about it while we walk back to the vehicles, I want to get the hell out of here."

Roy nodded his head and began to walk back towards the road. It was obvious that he was attempting to strike a deal with two duds. His opinion was based on the way they presented themselves and their overall appearance. Their eyes were bloodshot, probably from drinking excessively or from using drugs, and they wore strange clothes and long hair. Roy's assumptions were confirmed when he turned around to see if they were still following. Frank and Brett stood about fifty yards away, snorting cocaine out of the others hand with a straw while conversing about what they would do with their upcoming fortune.

They were obviously high when they reached the vehicle. Roy was standing next to his truck with a cell phone at his ear. They stood by their car wiping their noses as they tried to overhear Roy's conversation. Roy said "O.K." hung up the phone and approached the men with a very serious look on his face.

"I just spoke to my banker; the most I can get is $160,000 which is equal to $500 per acre. If acceptable I'll give you the money tomorrow morning."

The Florida pot heads didn't reply immediately but instead huddled together to consider the offer. Roy could hear them arguing and was able to determine that Frank was getting the upper hand, but he didn't know if that was beneficial or not. Frank, who was even more stoned than his sibling walked up to Roy with his hands on his hips.

"Alright man, we'll take $160,000 for it tomorrow but we need a $10,000 advance today for a total price of $170,000. We're almost out of cash."

Roy couldn't believe it and had a difficult time containing his excitement. He put his hand out with a modest smile.

"Ok, I'll make the arrangements today and we'll close tomorrow morning. Can I see the deed and your identification right now so that I can be sure that you are the true owners?" Brett dug around in the car until he found a manila envelope and then handed it to Roy. Inside was the Last Will and Testament of Seth Maki, a warranty deed that had been recorded in his grandson's names just days before, and a letter addressed to Frank and Brett. Everything seemed to be in order, but Roy would see a real estate attorney as soon as possible to verify the legitimacy of the deed. Frank showed his driver's license to Roy but Brett was not able to produce one because it had been revoked for driving while under the influence.

"Good enough. I'll meet you at your hotel this afternoon after I visit my bank and an attorney. I'll bring the $10,000 then."

Brett seemed somewhat antsy as he looked into his wallet.

"Do you have any cash you could float us right now? We're gonna celebrate this afternoon at the hotel and my credit cards are almost maxed out."

Roy had $80 in his wallet.

"Is this enough?"

"Yes that's enough for now. Thanks dude."

Brett informed Roy that they were staying at the Budget Host in Ishpeming, room 24. "I'll be there at about 4:00 p.m. today" Roy said as he stepped into his truck.

Roy couldn't get home fast enough. His mind was reeling with excitement and anxiety. He turned up the radio to a volume he had not exposed himself to since high school and began to sing just as loud. His favorite song, "Sherri Sherri" by Neil Diamond, rocked the truck. Roy didn't know most of the words but he sang anyway, he hadn't been this happy since the birth of his son and was not able to contain himself any longer. He reached for a pinch of Copenhagen, hoping that it would calm him down. It did and then Roy started to think about the letter from Seth Maki. The Finnish name Maki took up more space in the local phone book than any other so Roy was certain that the grandfather was a native "Yooper," meaning that he was originally from the Upper Peninsula. He speculated that Seth Maki had a daughter who moved to Florida and then married the father of the two dip shits that he was now attempting to buy the property from. Roy would have liked to read the letter but he was sure it would have made him feel badly about buying the land. It was probably a plea from a grandfather who greatly enjoyed and cherished the property, who in his time had walked and hunted every square foot of it a hundred times. Roy had noticed a very old deer blind overlooking the cedar swamp, built from the slabs produced by a portable saw mill. There was also a small spruce timber cabin on one of the ridges that was no longer usable because the roof had collapsed long before. Neither Frank nor Brett had noticed the deer blind or dilapidated cabin during their walk through the property, the only interest shown was related to the money that would fill their pockets after the resulting sale.

More than likely the letter had explained the value of the property in other terms, such as the wildlife that roamed the area and the trees that grew so perfectly because of the rich loam soils found there. Mr. Maki could have clear cut and sold the land to ensure a comfortable retirement but instead decided to hold it for his grandsons', hoping that they would enjoy it as he had and then pass it down to another generation when they perished. Roy surmised that Seth Maki must not have had a son and was not very close to his grandsons, otherwise he would have known that they would sell it as soon as it was given to them. What a shame. Roy was so disturbed by the greed, and so touched by the apparent love shown for the land by its' previous owner that he shut off his radio and decided to speak to the dead Seth Maki.

"Mr. Maki, I'm going to make a promise to you right now. If I'm able to pull this deal off, you have my word that I will cherish this land as you have. I will cut it conservatively to ensure that it always looks very good and I will not sell it, but rather pass it down to my family when I die."

With that said, the radio went back up to an almost intolerable level of volume and Roy began to sing loudly once again as his head bobbed up and down to "Cotton Eyed Joe". But as Roy's heart pumped with excitement, his mind was also filled with nerve racking anxiety. The phone call he had been on when the two men approached him at the property was a fake. He had not yet talked to the bank and was not at all certain that he would be loaned the money. The equity in his house was minimal, the payments on the skidder that he purchased for his logging business were astronomical and were funded by an impressive but unpredictable income that would diminish if he were to be hurt on the job, and his wife didn't work. Banks were typically apprehensive about vacant land as collateral so his other properties would not help his cause. Not to mention that he was the father of two children who consumed thousands of dollars in formula, diapers, clothes and food. Worth every penny though. And so in order to get the money, Roy would have to demonstrate that the land would immediately become an asset rather than a liability because he was paying much less than the actual worth.

As he drove down US 41 through West Ishpeming, Roy became

very optimistic while he contemplated the strategy that would be used to convince his banker. A single sustainable timber harvest on the land would produce enough money to easily pay it off. Most investors would cut it hard to recoup their initial investment and a large profit, but Roy firmly believed in and abided by the standards of sustainable forestry, knowing that it would also produce more profit over the long term. Roy knew of numerous investors, developers, and loggers who would jump at the chance to purchase the land for more than he would soon pay for it. They would cut the timber very hard and then subdivide the 320 acre parcel into many smaller pieces and then sell them for top dollar. He had seen this happen many times before, but this time Roy Gustafson would beat them to the punch. On this particular day, unlike the norm, Roy did not have a single negative thought prompted by his depression and he quietly thanked God for his optimism. He was certain that the anti-depressant medication was helping his outlook on life, the constant anxiety had somewhat diminished.

Roy's tires squealed as he made a sharp turn into the bank fifty minutes after departing from the land. He walked briskly past the tellers while saying hello and directly into the office of Brian Giroux, the Vice President of the National Savings Bank.

"I'm sorry to barge into your office like this Brian but I need a lot of money and I need it right now."

"That's O.K. Roy. What's going on?"

Roy sat down in front of Brian's desk with a very serious look on his face. There would be no small talk today.

"I just stumbled across a piece of land for sale, and I can buy it for less than half of what it's worth. I'm a damn good customer here Brian, never missed a payment on anything I own."

"You're definitely a wonderful customer Roy, I'll do whatever I can for you. How much do you need?"

"I need $170,000 by tomorrow morning."

Giroux sat back in his chair, situated his tie and folded his hands.

"That's a lot of money Roy."

Roy mostly spoke in words of a common Yooper and preferred to, but he had materialized an impressive arsenal of vocabulary because his mother had so often read to he and his brother as youngsters. This situation, like other business transactions that he took part in, warranted an intellectual approach and supportive justification.

"It is Brian, but one moderate harvest will earn enough capital to pay off the loan. Then I'll manage it as a working forest and subsequent cuts will render the land as a valuable asset rather than a financial liability, producing an average annual income of at least $40,000 over time. It's truly an opportunity of a lifetime."

Roy's statement provoked a change in Brian's posture from that of apprehension to curiousness, as he changed his seating from the back of his chair to the front.

"Why are they selling the property at such a reduced price?" he asked.

"Well, the sellers are from Florida so they have no concept of timber values, they initially were asking $800 per acre and I offered $500. Their names are Frank and Brett Richards and they recently inherited the land from their grandfather who I believe is originally from the area, his name was Seth Maki."

"Seth Maki?" Brian asked.

"Yes."

"I knew Seth, I've handled several loans for him over the last ten years or so. Smart man indeed, he's purchased numerous tracts of land throughout the central U.P. in addition to various rentals in Ishpeming, Marquette, and Negaunee. Seth Maki is a prime example of a successful man who made his money work for him rather than he being a slave to it. More importantly, he was a gem of a person. He and his late wife Julie raised three daughters in Negaunee and were well known for donating a great deal of their time and money to charity. Seth was a community leader."

"Wow. There must have been much more to the inheritance

than what the two Florida grandsons received" said Roy.

The nagging emotion of guilt for buying the land at a better than reasonable price had suddenly disappeared. There was no doubt that Seth Maki had many other properties that were as or more valuable than this land, these were probably given to his daughters and other grandchildren.

"What do you say Brian?"

Roy was staring at him, anxiously waiting for an answer.

"Well Roy, if it were a year ago I'd hand you a cashier's check right now, but since we were overtaken by National Savings Bank I am required to get approval from our corporate office in Iowa before granting a loan of more than $100,000."

Brian turned to the computer to access Roy's account information. After looking at the screen for a few minutes he turned back to Roy.

"I want to be honest with you up front Roy. Even though I personally have no doubt about your ability to pay back the loan, the corporate office will question it because your debt ratio is presently near the allowable limit."

Roy looked to the floor and searched his mind for a way to lower the so called "debt ratio".

"What about the other vacant land that I own? I realize that I have a different loan for these but they are worth much more than I owe because of the timber on them."

Brian nodded his head with a sympathetic look.

"I understand what you're saying but the timber is considered by banks to have no value until it is cut and sold. The assessed value of the land is the same whether it has merchantable timber on it or not. If our Board of Trustees still existed here in Ishpeming they would certainly agree with your contentions, but because the corporate office is now in Iowa and because the corporate loan guidelines are strictly adhered to...."

"That's bullshit" interrupted Roy.

"Are you telling me I'm going to be turned down?"

"Hold on Roy. I'm going to contact a coordination banker in

Iowa right now, I'll have an answer for you within the hour."

Roy stood up and reluctantly shook Brian Giroux's hand.

"I want you to inform the coordination banker that if National Savings does not grant this loan, they'll be less one damn good customer. My accounts will be closed and moved elsewhere within 24 hours."

"I'll let them know Roy, I sure would hate to lose you over this."

"I'd hate to lose you as my banker Brian, but my loyalty to you cannot continue if National Savings isn't loyal to me. I think the people that own these banks are more than eager to lend money for an item that loses value every year, such as a car. But they are unwilling to lend money for something that will actually make the borrower some capital, such as this land that I want to buy. I wish this place was still the good old Miner's Bank, it was a much better establishment back then."

"I wish it were too" responded Brian.

Roy had made his point, he walked out of the bank with little confidence remaining.

Instead of driving home to his wife who would provide no sympathy or show any interest for that matter, he traveled to a woman's home who would listen carefully to every word that came out of his mouth. When he walked in the door she was making a pie made from blueberries that were picked the previous summer.

"Hi Love" she exclaimed with a smile.

Sarah Gustafson had always provided Roy with the affection that Kaylie forbid him in his own home. Roy considered his mother to be a selfless angel, a perfect wife and mother who could not be compared to anyone he had ever met. His own wife could not even begin to fill her shoes, and at this point Roy was quite certain she never would.

Roy sat down with his mom over a cup of coffee and a snack of Trenary toast, a U.P made cinnamon toast, and explained the day's events so far. His father overheard the conversation and sat down at the table with a piece of Trenary toast already in his hand. Roy had hoped his dad would not become involved in the conversation because of his strong "old school" opinion about borrowing money. Roy was surprised that Robert listened to nearly the entire story before he made his opinion known.

"I never took out a loan in my life. A person shouldn't buy something unless they have the money in their savings account." he blurted out.

"You young people are foolish to borrow so much money for fancy houses and vehicles, you're going to work for at least ten years just to pay the interest back to those crooks at the bank. Land is way overpriced now a days, I would never pay that much for 320 acres. You've got a family to support and you'll have all you can do to pay the taxes on the deer camp when I'm dead, this should be your priority."

Roy shook his head.

"You're wrong dad. You of all people should know the value of timber and vacant land. After all, you taught Gage and me much of what we know about it. How the hell would you expect me to save $160,000 in cash? The value of timber on that land is tremendous, I saw some Bird's Eye maple this morning and that stuff is worth its' weight in gold."

Robert was about to respond again when Sarah spoke.

"I think you're right Roy, you are a very smart businessman and you've done very well for yourself at a young age. But if the bank won't back you up you'll just have to let it go. There's nothing else you can do sweetheart."

Roy got up and walked to the phone to call the bank. Forty minutes had passed since he left the bank and he wanted to know if the verdict was in.

"I'm sorry Roy, we can only approve a loan for $30,000, your debt to equity ratio is just too high right now. Would they consider a land contract with $30,000 down?"

Roy didn't need to tell his parents what the answer was, it was written all over his face. He hung up the phone without answering the Vice President's question, put on his jacket and walked towards the door without saying anything more to his parents.

"Eh Roy" yelled his father in an attempt to stop him.

"I've got to get back to work now" Roy replied as he closed the door. He jumped into his truck and drove towards the hotel where the Richards' were staying. Roy was disgusted with the bank and swore to himself that he would be their customer no longer. He was so distraught by the lost opportunity to own such a fine piece of property that he was forced to choke back tears as he pulled into the hotel parking lot. The cell phone rang. He didn't want to answer but he thought it might be his wife.

"Hello."

"I was talking to you when you walked out of my door." It was his father.

"I don't feel much like talking right now dad."

Roy assumed that his dad had called to move him forward in his usual tactless manner.

"I'll borrow you the money, I've already arranged for it at my bank."

Roy was speechless.

"You're mother and I are going to need it back in a year or so, we're on a fixed income you know. Meet me at the Ishpeming Community Bank in five minutes."

"Dad you don't need to do this."

His father had already hung up.

Robert Gustafson had raised his sons to be honest and hardworking and he trusted Roy's analysis of the property, even though a substantial sum of money was at risk. Robert had also been a businessman in his younger days. Upon graduation from high school in his home town of Ishpeming, he was immediately escorted by his father to the Cleveland Cliffs "Shaft" iron ore mine. As a young man Robert had dreamed of starting his very own construction and masonry business, but the dangerous and well paid occupation of underground mining was his father's choice for him. He worked in various underground mines in the Ishpeming area for seventeen years, until finally the grueling shift work and his persistent dream caused him to start his own business. It would turn out to be one of the best decisions of his life, the Gustafson & Sons Construction Company became very successful and owned dozens of rental properties over a period of decades until Robert retired at the age of 59. Gage and Roy worked for their father as young men and were taught the value of a dollar bill, and were also adamantly forced to become tremendous physical laborers. Despite Robert's hope of his sons taking over the business when he retired, neither of them was interested in doing so.

Roy was propelled to a mood equivalent to the sellers, who were both as high as a kite in the hotel. He met his father at the bank where a cashier's check was waiting for him in the amount of $160,000 in addition to $10,000 in cash for the advancement. Roy then gave authorization to the Ishpeming Community Bank manager to transfer all of his accounts and loans from the National Savings Bank. He and his father walked out of the bank together.

"I don't know how to thank you dad. I promise you won't regret this. I'll have the money back to you plus interest in eight months at the latest."

"Don't worry about the interest. I've got no doubt that you've made a wise decision. Your mom says I give you and Gage a hard time too often, maybe she's right."

Roy hugged his dad, bid him farewell and made off towards his truck. Robert stood there for a moment while watching his eldest son drive away, enjoying a moment of pride.

Roy made a short stop at his attorney's office to confirm that Frank and Brett Richards owned the property outright, and then proceeded on to the hotel. The pair was in the shape that Roy expected when he arrived, both were drunk and the smell of marijuana was almost overwhelming. The room was already a mess, empty beer cans and fast food containers littered the floor and Roy noticed a syringe on the bed side table. Because of the two characters he was dealing with in this matter, Roy would continue to worry until a warranty deed was placed in his hand on the following day.

"Did you bring the advance?" Frank asked in a serious tone.

"Yes."

Roy pulled out an envelope and placed it on the table. He wanted to depart from the hotel as quickly as possible, after realizing that if the police were to walk in at that moment they would be convinced that a drug deal was underway.

"I'll meet you tomorrow morning at Attorney Graywood's office, 10:00 a.m. sharp. It's across from Buck's Sub Shop downtown."

"What's your hurry? Do you want a beer?" asked Brett in a drunken and unfriendly tone. "No thanks, I need to get home to the kids."

"Can you hook us up with some whores tonight?"

"I don't know of any establishments like that around here."

"What the fuck do people do for fun around here? This place is a bore."

Roy had been offended by, and immediately disliked Brett Richards the very first time he laid eyes on him earlier that morning. But he refrained from saying anything to anger him, there was far too much at stake.

"I'm sorry you feel that way. We rely on people from out of town to boost our economy. I would suggest eating at the Venice Supper Club tonight, they have excellent Italian food and a very friendly atmosphere. Afterwards you could have a drink there or you may want to stop by Jack's Tee Pee or the Congress for a beer. You might get lucky and run into a couple of nice girls around town."

"Thanks bud, we'll do that," said Frank as he laid on one of the beds, seemingly ready to pass out.

"Did you know our grandfather Seth Maki?"

"No, I didn't."

Brett poured himself a shot and offered another to Roy with a hand gesture. Roy reached for the door knob.

"No thanks."

Roy thought that Brett Richards was becoming more and more unlikeable by the minute. "You know," said Brett "the cheap bastard was a millionaire and that's all he gave us was this lousy land out in the middle of bum fuck Egypt."

"I'm sorry to hear that Brett, I'll see you fella's tomorrow morning at 10:00 a.m." "Alright man, we'll be there and we expect to see a check for $160,000 or we are going to have a serious problem with you."

Roy did not respond. It was a blatant threat but he overcame the urge to reciprocate with poor manners and instead exited the hotel room. It was obvious to Roy that Brett Richards had a mean streak in him.

Roy hadn't cut a stick of timber for the day but he was exhausted anyway. He looked forward to an evening of reading and snuggling with his children. During the drive he wondered how Brett and Frank Richards could materialize into such worthlessness. With $170,000 in their hands, Roy was certain that Brett and Frank would end up dead or in jail before too long, especially Brett. Roy thought Brett was capable of just about anything, and was tempted to call the Ishpeming Police after the warranty deed was signed. Roy was hoping they would stay at the hotel for the night, otherwise they might be picked up for drunk driving or possession of narcotics. This would definitely postpone or even ruin the deal. Roy was excited when he arrived at home. He greeted the children and then told his wife about the property. Kaylie's only interest was to escape from home for bowling league that night.

"I wish I could just run around looking at land all day." she said.

Roy expected nothing better from her.

The following morning Roy was relieved to see Frank and Brett Richards at the lawyer's office at 10:15 a.m., they were as anxious as he to close the deal. Everything went off without a hitch. A warranty deed was recorded at the Marquette County courthouse and the money was transferred from escrow to the two losers from Florida. Roy promised himself that he would turn them into authorities if he witnessed any more illegal activity, but he did not hear from them again. Roy found out later they had purchased a brand new Ford Explorer from Twin City Ford before skipping town that afternoon.

Within seven months, Roy had made a very selective cut on the Maki property which provided enough money to pay back his father, and also a significant amount of cash which he placed into his savings account. Roy also gave his mom and dad an additional sum equivalent to ten percent in interest. The timber was loaded with Bird's Eye maple, which was a defect that increased the value of such logs by substantial portions. That particular land purchase was by far the greatest investment he had ever made, or ever would in the future.

Chapter Six

Things were looking up for Gage Gustafson. His job, although sometimes monotonous, was going very well and he was feeling much like himself again. Much of his free time was spent in the woods enjoying the hobbies that he had for most of his life, while seriously contemplating the future. Gage was able to clear his head while alone and pondered many productive ideas. He re-visited the advice given to him by his loved ones but became frustrated for overthinking. He reassured himself that he must enjoy his current situation and that difficult decisions would be made in good time.

The bars of Ishpeming were visited only occasionally and Gage kept his drinking to a minimum unless Dave and other friends joined him for a night at camp. There at the camp men were free to drink and behave as they wished, exhibiting childlike responsibility without any threat of repercussion.

The month of June had finally arrived after a tremendously brutal winter. The stream levels were now at elevations that would entice brook trout fisherman, and Gage didn't waste any time getting started. Before daybreak on a Saturday morning, Gage picked up his cousin John and brother Roy and they traveled west to a favorite stretch of water near the village of Nestoria. A rugged two track logging road, partially grown over with young conifers, served as a deterrent to most fishermen who owned large trucks that were nicely cared for. But Gage owned a 1991 Chevy S-10 pick-up truck that crawled through such roads with ease, the constant scratches from the young trees and brush didn't bother him at all. The two-track ended at an old landing that was once used for decking timber and was a perfect place to park. With Gage in the lead, the three men walked to the north strapped with wicker creels, rods, and small buckets filled with dace minnows. They wore old clothes that were used only for these adventures because any better clothes or waders would be ruined by such terrain. The walk to the stream was only 1/8 of a mile in distance but it took nearly forty minutes to get there due to the thick mud and dense wall of tag alder brush above it. But when they arrived the mere site of the river made their trip worthwhile; the water cascaded through large rocks into a narrow but very long stretch of deep water, and the forest that surrounded the stream corridor had recently transformed into a most beautiful shade of green with the onset of the growing season.

The Gustafson men were well known for their addiction to brook trout fishing. At about the age of six, Gage began to follow his father, brother and cousin John to either hunt or fish in areas near their beloved camp. No matter how far they walked, he dare not complain for fear of being left at home for the next trip. The small streams and surrounding landscape of the area presented a physical challenge which deterred most fishermen from courting the elusive brook trout. Most would rather fish by boat in one of the numerous lakes found in any direction from town. But not the Gustafson's. The relentless onslaught launched by mosquitos and the quagmire of tag alder brush associated with most streams were expected and embraced, for they were the primary reasons that solitude was easily found near such waters. And once these obstacles were overcome, all that remained was paradise; paradise in the form of a twelve inch brook trout attacking a lively minnow at the end of a six foot rod.

The three men fished separately but within view of one another, speaking only to themselves unless a dandy was placed in the creel. John was the first to catch a fish and also the first to throw modesty aside.

"Look at this one Roy, he's almost fourteen inches," said John as he held a fat bellied brook trout up while standing on a slate rock at the stream's edge.

"I guess it's my day today, I got five and you guys only have two between you."

Roy congratulated John with no sense of jealousy in his voice.

But Gage was a bit more competitive than Roy and did not take kindly to John's bragging, even though he was his favorite cousin. John continued to brag to Roy how it was he and not Mr. John Voelker, the renowned author and fisherman, who was the greatest trout fisherman the U.P. had ever seen. Gage finally decided that he couldn't handle it anymore so he quietly snuck up behind John as he boasted about himself. When John stopped talking for a moment to bend down to place the mount worthy trout into his creel, Gage gently placed his foot on the small of John's back and then pushed hard when John attempted to rise. The result was comparable to a grasshopper leap, John flew up and out over the river before plunging into the dark water below. Roy and Gage laughed ferociously while John scampered about in an attempt to recover his equipment and fish.

After the men filled their creels with more than their legal limit of brook trout and could no longer fend off the overwhelming attack of mosquitoes and deer flies, they journeyed back to the truck and drove to camp where they were joined by friends for a night of cards, saunas, stories, and beer. These were the types of outings that Gage Gustafson lived for. He did not think about anything particularly important that weekend and instead enjoyed trout fishing, camp entertainment and meaningless conversation with Dave and other friends.

The following Monday was an important day for Gage. He had been employed at Tasson Distributing Company for three months and was now eligible to participate in the 401(k) retirement plan. This excited him more than it would most others because he was very much interested in the stock market. His father had taught he and Roy about investing and saving money at an early age, and both contributed monthly to an IRA that consisted of stocks and bonds. Now Gage would have the opportunity to choose and invest in dozens of mutual funds, for which the company would partially match his contribution. The employee's accounts were set up and managed by 1st Street Financial, and Gage was to meet with a planner that morning to set up his very own portfolio. The financial planner, named Bart Collins, was very impressed with Gage's knowledge of the stock market. Gage inquired with a number of questions regarding no load funds, performance history, and expense ratios, some of which Collins could not readily answer. Gage was equally impressed with Bart Collins, he was dressed sharply and he carried himself in a very professional manner. He explained to Gage how he came to be in his current position and how he prepared himself to get there. Bart had worked hard at Northern Michigan University to obtain a degree in Finance and found plenty of jobs available after graduation. He began in an entry level position in the Lower Peninsula and eventually worked his way back to Ishpeming and started his own firm some years later. It was immediately obvious to Gage that Bart was a vastly successful businessman, and his mind kicked into high gear as ideas returned to him.

After the account was set up and the bi-weekly contribution decided upon, Bart Collins asked questions of Gage that unintentionally forced him to look more closely at his current situation with newborn scrutiny. Gage realized that his job as a deliveryman, or salesman for that matter, may not be enough to keep him satisfied for thirty years. It was a good job, but Gage began to wonder if there was something else that might suit him better. Until recently, Gage was relatively certain that he would spend his life working at the warehouse, enjoying his free time with family and friends while residing in Ishpeming. Not anymore. After only three months of employment his mind was telling him that maybe his career desires would not be met at

Tasson Distributing Company. This troubled Gage as he could not understand why things were suddenly changing after being totally content earlier that morning, after escaping his thoughts for the weekend. The dream of becoming a Wildlife Biologist with the Michigan Department of Natural Resources had faded because Gage thought that college was no longer the place for him. But maybe he was just not meant to be a Wildlife Biologist. Maybe he was more interested in becoming a financial planner of some sort. After all, he would be throwing three years of college away if he did not return to get a degree. During his route that day Gage was emerged in deep thought, attempting to figure out which path was most suitable for him while recalling the advice of his godmother. The possibilities of becoming a salesman for the company seemed more realistic now after Mike Tasson had talked with him about it just days before, but Gage wasn't sure that such a position was suitable for him either. Gage drove straight to his mother's house after work that evening, he needed to seek her opinion after explaining his thoughts.

Sarah Gustafson was painting an old bookshelf when Gage arrived. She had been retired for ten years after a serious car accident almost claimed her life and left her with aching bones, but she always found something productive to do at home.

"Hi love, are you hungry?"

"Yah I could eat, thanks Ma."

Sarah scurried into the kitchen to heat a fresh pot of soup for Gage and herself.

"How are you sweetheart? I'm glad you stopped by for a visit."

"I'm good mom, but I need to talk to you about work."

Gage wanted to confide in his father also; no doubt that he would be interested in what Gage had to say. Gage yelled downstairs for him but there was no answer.

"He's gone fishing again Gage, he missed a big one yesterday and he went back to get him."

Gage smiled. His father was obsessed with brook trout; the hobby ensured that the sixty-six year old would act as though he was only thirty during fishing season. Sarah's only complaint about her husband's fishing excursions were that he would sometimes fall into a relapse for several days afterward, and she would have to wait on him until he recovered, only to watch him rush off to the stream once again.

Gage ate two bowls of his mother's delicious soup accompanied by her homemade bread before describing his issue. As always, she sat quietly and listened to him explain the new development in his mind. She was pleasantly surprised with what he had to say, especially regarding the prospect of returning to college to finish his degree.

"There's no doubt that you need to go back to college Gage. But if you are still not certain what field should be chosen, then you should wait for a confident decision."

This was serious business for Mrs. Gustafson. Since the car accident long before, her only priority had been the well-being of her family. She was worried that her son would return to college with confusion still lingering about him, which may cause him to drop out once again. If this happened, there was a good chance that he would never again return to obtain a degree. She remembered the difficult decisions made as a young woman in California. Raised by a hard working family on a dairy ranch near Santa Rosa, Sarah longed to attend college after high school. Her mother's name was Agnes Boschi, an immigrant direct from Italy who demanded that Sarah stay on the ranch and work like the rest of the family. After some time had passed, Sarah was even more determined to attend college to become a nurse. Even though her mother informed her that she would no longer be welcome at the ranch if she left for these "selfish" reasons, Sarah attended nursing school and earned a degree as a Registered Nurse. Her mother felt so betrayed that she refused to even speak to Sarah, but Sarah knew in her heart that she wanted to live the American dream. She eventually patched up her mother's anger and then met Gage's father while he was stationed at a military base in California.

Many years later at forty-nine years of age, she was a nursing supervisor at the Mather Nursing home when a drunk driver struck her while she ran an errand in Marquette. She barely survived the accident and was confined to the intensive care unit at Marquette General hospital for six months. Even though her long term injuries prevented her from working any longer, she carried a positive attitude and concentrated totally on raising her children.

"It was God's plan," she would say.

Fortunately Gage didn't need to make a decision immediately. He tried to convince himself to enjoy the next month of summer before the fall semester enrollment deadline in August. Before driving to his apartment that night he decided to visit his brother and the kids, anxious to speak with Roy about potentially returning to college. Gage opened the door without knocking and immediately regretted doing so. The annoying screams of Kaylie filled the air of the otherwise comfortable and beautiful home. Roy was standing in the living room with his back to the door with one child in his arms and the other attached to his leg, pleading with Kaylie to calm down. Kaylie was in the kitchen doing what she did best, complaining. She bitched about the housework and the constant pressure that the kids placed on her. Gage announced his presence and surprised Roy, who in turn yelled to Kaylie.

"Gage is here."

She walked through the room and out the door without welcoming Gage or bidding farewell to her family, off to the bars once again.

"Sorry to barge in like that Roy, I was..."

"It's alright Gage."

Roy watched as his wife slammed the door and then directed his attention to Khora and Otto as they leaped into the arms of his brother. This brought a hesitant smile to Roy's face. He sat down on the couch and put his left hand to his forehead as Gage hugged the kids and then sent them into another room after awhile.

"I don't know what to do for her anymore."

It was the first time Roy had openly acknowledged a problem with his marriage.

"I just can't seem to make her happy Gage. She doesn't want to be home, she doesn't want to work, and she sure as hell doesn't want to spend time with me. I figure I'm pretty damn understanding about the free time, all I ask is for her to be a good mother."

Gage looked at his brother with sympathy.

"It's not your fault Roy."

"But I won't give up Gage, I love her and I won't give up."

After awhile Roy's mood improved as he watched Gage play dress up with the kids. Khora insisted that Gage wear her elastic skirt and truffles. She was kind enough to place her princess crown on his head, making him look like a gay prince from the Stone Age. Gage didn't mind.

Before he went on his way later that evening, Gage told Roy about the meeting with the financial planner and how he now questioned whether he should stay at Tasson's or return to NMU.

"I have an idea," said Roy.

"Why don't you go up to Michigan Technological University in Houghton for a couple of years and get a degree in Forestry? I've got five full-time employees now and I'm working on another land deal. I could use a good Forester to manage the land and arrange for other acquisitions. We would be a great team. If things go as I expect we'll have to hire a land manager within a year or two anyway. I can barely keep up with all of it and I'm not very proficient at marking timber or other things that Foresters do. What do you say?"

"Gosh I don't know Roy, I need to get through this confusion. I'll think about it though, thanks for the offer."

Like all human beings Gage Gustafson had faults. His most prevalent fault was the inability to make timely decisions. He thought about things again and again and after finally making a decision, he was still uncertain that he made the right choice. Going out for supper with him could turn into an all-night affair. He would study the menu for at least twenty minutes before narrowing down his preference to three items. He would then discuss the choices with whomever accompanied him to the restaurant and when he found out what they would order he would become even more confused. The problem would be dramatically intensified when a major decision was set in front of him, such as where he should go fishing on any given day. Friends would complain that after driving a fair distance towards a stream, Gage would pull over without warning and then move on to a location in an entirely different direction. All because he simply could not decide which stream was the better choice that day.

Another fault that enraged people, even more than his indecisiveness, was a habit that caused him to lose himself during a conversation. If someone spoke for an extended period of time or if he was not particularly interested in what they had to say, Gage would drift off into his own little world. A blank stare would come over his face as he escaped to another place to think about a more interesting topic or more urgent problem, his mother called this place "Gage Land". She would scold him every time she noticed him looking through someone rather than being attentive enough to listen to what they had to say.

"That is very rude Gage."

Chapter Seven

At that particular moment in his life, Gage was experiencing a natural dilemma that all young adults must confront. Many college students did not declare a major until their junior year, they first concentrated on liberal studies that were required by any curriculum and then based their decision on the classes enjoyed the most. Gage contemplated his options over the next week, doing so most intently while fishing after work. For a reason unknown to him, he did very poorly on the streams every night which made him realize that life would go on if he had to leave his beloved Upper Peninsula. Becoming a stock broker or financial planner in a mid-sized city became more appealing by the day, and he set an appointment to meet an advisor on July 12th. His visit to the Northern Michigan University campus brought back memories, some pleasant and a few that stung a bit.

Gage had a long list of items to ask the advisor including the question of how long it would take for him to graduate with a bachelor's degree in Business or Finance. He hadn't been on campus since September of the year before and he felt much like a different person now. The break had given him a chance to discontinue his dependency on Sherri Anderson and to become a more independent and responsible person. He was also much more mature and confident after conquering the slump that he shoved himself into. The insecurities that young men and women feel during high school and the first couple years in college no longer distracted him, and he was now ready to return with no worries of failure. After his brother gave him a gentle beating in the Rainbow Bar some months earlier, Gage had also started working out almost every night at the Strength and Fitness Gym in Ishpeming which led him to be in the best physical shape of his life. His self-confidence was soaring.

The meeting with the advisor went very well and only took an hour. Gage took notes as Mr. Troy Morton of the College of Business gave him advice. Mr. Morton pointed out that if Gage piled up on the core business courses in proper sequence during the fall, winter, and summer semesters, he could feasibly graduate in August of 1996. Fortunately Gage had completed most of the required liberal classes and he had also taken three lower level business classes through his junior year. Mr. Morton described such courses as *Business Management, Investment Banking*, and *Stock/Bond Investing*, which excited Gage greatly. The titles of those classes sounded much better than *Animal Physiology, Zoology 2, Advanced Biometrics*, and *Statistical Population Model Interpretation;* these were the courses that Gage faced in his senior year as a Wildlife Biology major. Furthermore, a degree in Biology would not even remotely guarantee a job in the natural resource field, the graduate placement for the program was only 47%. And that statistic included seasonal employees. A bachelor's degree in Finance, on the other hand, bolstered a placement of 93% with an average annual income beginning at $33,000.

The meeting with Troy Morton made it very clear to Gage that he would now change his major to Finance and begin coursework in late August. He walked directly to the registrar's office to enroll in the classes that he had been advised to sign up for. Indecisiveness plagued him no longer, Gage knew what he wanted to do.

Gage shared the news with his family and employer on the following day, both of which supported his decision enthusiastically. He would continue to work at the warehouse until the fall semester commenced and would then work part time loading trucks as studies allowed. His parents wanted him to come back to their home to stay until he graduated but Gage decided to stay at the apartment. He enjoyed the independence and felt more like a responsible adult living at his own place. It was good for his confidence. The following year and a half would be a financially difficult time, his parents had paid for his tuition up to that point but Gage would pay for the remainder himself by obtaining college loans. And so Gage Gustafson had returned to a path that could potentially lead to success and long term happiness. But he would have to work hard to get it done this time.

That night Gage heard a knock on his door.

"Oh, hi Dave, how are you chum?"

Dave was obviously intoxicated as he entered the apartment with a half-ass smile, after visiting a bar nearby.

"Where the hell have you been Gage?"

"I've been working Dave, trying to figure some things out."

"Well I've been trying to figure things out too Gage, and you're nowhere to be found."

"I'm right here Dave, easy to find unless you're looking for me at the bar."

"I need to get the fuck out of here Gage. My girlfriend broke up with me, I lost my shitty part-time job and I'm nearly broke. To make matters worse, my best friend is avoiding me."

Gage put his arm around Dave and walked him to the couch.

"I'm not avoiding you pal. I'm just trying to get my shit straight. We're adults now Dave."

Gage made coffee and the two childhood friends confided in one another for a very long time. Dave had always been there for Gage, especially after the break-up with Sherri Anderson. And even though Dave was not advancing himself Gage had a great deal of faith in his best friend, and attempted to prompt him to consider changes during that long conversation. Before Dave departed, Gage hugged him and made him promise to stay away from the bars for a while. Dave agreed reluctantly and also promised Gage that he would begin looking for a full-time job the following day. Very few people saw any potential in Dave but his close friend had faith that he would indeed become a successful adult.

Chapter Eight

The months of July and August during the year of 1995 passed by quickly. Gage worked all of the overtime offered to him and picked up a second job as a bartender at no other than the Rainbow Bar. Each Saturday he worked a sixteen hour shift at the bar which started at 11:00 a.m. and ended at 3:00 a.m. on Sunday morning. He came to be known by his first name by the regular patrons, and developed into a very good bartender after learning the duties required by the job. There was no need to master the trade of exotic mixed drinks and margaritas because there were no requests for such fancy beverages in Ishpeming. Any given customer would likely order a beer or a simple mixed drink such as a brandy and coke. Bartending was both an interesting and demanding job. By 3:00 a.m. on Sunday mornings, Gage would be totally worn out after serving dozens of customers, breaking up at least two scraps, and cleaning the bar after close. It was not unusual for him to sleep until mid afternoon on Sunday, only to wake up to a hangover inflicted by second hand smoke. Sunday afternoons and evenings were his to enjoy, as he normally traveled south of town for a productive visit to a dependable stretch of trout stream with his dad, brother or cousin John.

Gage came to appreciate his family and life much more after working at the bar for a few weeks. Some of the patrons had settled for a life that consisted of a forty-hour week at minimum wage and a weekend spent at the bar rather than with their children. Gage was saddened to learn that more people than he realized were hopelessly addicted to alcohol, their sense of happiness and integrity falsely portrayed only during a visit to the bar. But there were also many responsible people that occasionally stopped by for a few drinks, their happiness fueled only by a productive lifestyle and Gage learned much during conversations with them. He also met several Ishpeming natives that had since moved away to capitalize on career aspirations but returned to their beloved home town each year. Doctors, lawyers, business owners and hard-working blue collar tradesmen all inspired Gage as he listened to their stories of success.

When school began in August of 1995, Gage continued to work on a limited basis at the bar and warehouse but concentrated almost totally on his studies. And study he did. He was determined to earn good grades and graduate at the end of the following summer. Gage had become very frugal with his money and had managed to save enough to help with many of his weekly expenses. His mother kept the refrigerator and freezer stocked with prepared meals that could be heated up when he returned from school, which he appreciated very much. Gage tackled the challenges of college head on and was earning straight "A's" after the month of September had passed.

While studying outside of Jamrich Hall on a gorgeous fall afternoon, Gage heard a familiar voice say hello from behind him. He turned to see Sherri Anderson, dressed in nicely fitting blue jeans and a tee shirt.

"How are you Gage? It's good to see you back at school."

Gage was more than a bit nervous to see Sherri but he was able to retain his composure.

"I'm fine Sherri, How are you doing?" Gage asked as though he had spoken to her the day before.

"I'm doing alright I guess. I took a break from college but now I'm back. I've called you a few times and I also sent you a letter months ago. Did you read it?"

"Nope."

Sherri was stunned by Gage's answer; he didn't even look at her when he responded.

"Gage, I know you probably hate me for what I did to you, but I want you to know that I'm very sorry. I loved you Gage, but I didn't realize it until after that night at the party."

Gage finally looked directly into Sherri's eyes with a very serious expression on his face. "You loved me? You were dating another guy while seeing me and you have the gall to say you loved me? I went through hell after that night Sherri. I couldn't concentrate on anything and I was drinking all the time. But now I'm back on top of things, and being ashamed of the way I reacted to your stunt has made me a stronger person, much stronger."

Tears were rolling down Sherri's face as she took one step closer.

"I broke things off with him after realizing what I had done. I can't tell you how sorry I am for what I've put you through."

She paused for a moment to write something on a torn piece of paper.

"Here's my phone number. I would love to take you out for dinner sometime."

A part of Gage wanted to take the number from Sherri and begin again where they had left off, but his pride would not allow it. Instead, he packed his books, stood up and began to walk away. He had no trust left in him for Sherri Anderson and refused to rebuild it.

"Give it to someone else."

Roy Gustafson was similar to Gage in many ways but very different in others. He was very tolerant of the misgivings of other people, especially those of his wife. He continued to put a great deal of effort into his marriage and children, but only a portion was paying off. His relationship with Kaylie was weakening by the day despite his unique abilities to understand her problems. His battle with depression continued, aided by the anti-depressant that he took daily.

October arrived with a decrease in temperatures but an increase in the testosterone among men of the U.P. It was the official beginning of autumn and most outdoorsmen would prefer the month of October over any other. Ducks, geese, grouse, and deer were among the animals sought after. Most of the rustic camps were opened for the first time since deer season ended on November 30th of the year before. Many landowners stayed at their camp every weekend throughout the fall and early winter. There was much to do before deer season opened on November 15th, and the Gustafson men were passionately loyal to their woodsy obsessions. Each weekend was consumed by hunting, cutting firewood, scouting for deer and other enjoyable hobbies while residing at the deer camp. Most of the fine ladies of the Upper Peninsula really did not understand the need for their husbands to leave them and their children stranded on the weekends, but accepted it because of the long standing tradition involved.

Roy welcomed the fifty and sixty degree temperatures of early October after suffering through much warmer weather throughout the summer. His occupation as a logger required him to work hard no matter what the element and he greatly preferred cold weather over warm. Because of his work ethic and strong nose for timber-land real estate, his small company was booming. He now had seven dedicated employees who either cut timber by hand or ran harvesting equipment that produced a large volume of wood. Roy was buying or selling land on a monthly basis, profits were used to purchase more land at a price far less than he knew it to be worth. Many realtors had no concept of timber value so he was able to offer a price that was much less than asked, and the bid would sometimes be accepted. Roy intended to keep his promise to the dead Seth Maki and enjoyed spending time on that 320 acre parcel more than any other.

A typical Saturday in October at the Gustafson deer camp consisted of an early breakfast of bacon and eggs, a short drive to a block of state land near the Black River, and about five hours of walking behind a bird dog. The dog was a three year old wire-haired pointer named Bracken, who was well trained for the retrieval of waterfowl and the more complicated hunt of ruffed grouse. If a bag were put over his head Bracken was a fine looking animal. But his face resembled a terrier which prompted most people to believe he was a mutt. Bracken was named after the common Bracken fern, found in most places where grouse could be sought after successfully with a good wing-shooter following. The dog was owned by Roy but his father and brother used him almost whenever they pleased. Bracken was an unusually versatile dog equipped with a nose that could seek out grouse no matter what the weather, and an adamantly loyal personality that suited him well as a house dog. Hunters lined up within twenty yards of each other and walked slowly in a cardinal direction through thick aspen and young conifer. They would keep an eye on the dog or listen for his bell if he was beyond their sight as he moved through the aspen saplings with his nose to the ground. When the scent of a bird was discovered, whether it be a grouse or woodcock, he would stop in his tracks and raise his right foreleg. Or he would continue to creep after the scent until the bird flushed. Shots would be fired shortly after, but either way the majority of the blasts would be unsuccessful because grouse were only a blur during flight.

During each week Gage continued to concentrate on his coursework throughout October but worked significantly less to free up some time for hunting. His mind was like a sponge which absorbed most of the information provided by the classes he was enrolled in. He was very interested in the topics covered. He could now see himself as a respected financial advisor who provided reliable and timely service to his clients. Gage had formulated a plan for after graduation, he would take a job wherever necessary and then move back to the area after he became experienced. His long term goal was to someday own his own firm in Ishpeming, just like Bart Collins had done.

Chapter Nine

On a cool evening in late October, Gage was seated at his desk in the apartment staring at the wall in deep thought about whitetail bucks in rut. Deer season was just over two weeks away and like many other hunters in the U.P., Gage was having a difficult time thinking of anything else. The daydream was interrupted by a knock on the door and the entrance of Roy and his children. It was a pleasant surprise as they had not visited Gage at the apartment since he moved in. Roy had deer season on his mind as well, and the brothers talked about it for at least an hour while playing around with the kids.

Roy then told Gage a disturbing story about the two men that he purchased the 320 acre block of land from near the Fence Grade. Roy had been on the land cruising timber and scouting for deer alone that morning. When he returned to his truck the Richards' were waiting for him, sitting on the hood of a Ford Explorer. As Roy approached within 100 yards he could see the Florida license plate and immediately knew who the owners of the vehicle were. Frank and Brett Richards both smiled reluctantly as Roy shook their hands and asked why they had returned to the U.P.

"Well," said Brett, "we came back because we figure you owe us some money."

Roy looked the two men over. They were both obviously high on something and their appearance had worsened since the last time he had met with them.

"What are you talking about?" Roy asked.

Frank looked at his brother Brett for a response. Brett pulled out a piece of paper from his pocket with a name and phone number written on it, and held it up for Roy to see.

"Do you know this logger?"

"Yah, I know who Eric Fredy is. He owns a large logging company out of Negaunee. Why do you ask?"

Roy was starting to feel uncomfortable as Frank stepped forward and stared at him with a not so friendly expression on his face.

"Before we met you that morning at the gas station, we put a hand written advertisement for the land on the billboard in the store. This Fredy fellow called my cell phone soon after we walked the property with you, he left a message stating that he was very interested in the land. I told him to go and look right away and to call me back that night if he could offer us more than you had."

Roy had no idea where Frank Richard's story was going and he was becoming more confused by the minute. He expressed his confusion by saying "O.K?" sarcastically, before Frank continued with the story.

"Anyway, he did call us back that night but we never got the message, we didn't find out about the message until just a few days ago when he somehow tracked down our phone number in Florida. He wanted to find out if the land was still for sale."

Roy was becoming impatient, he had better things to do than listening to a drug addict. "Where the hell are you going with this?" he asked.

"Why don't you shut up and listen" Brett blurted out after toking off of what looked to be a joint. Roy turned towards Brett and then looked back at Frank as he continued.

"Fredy said he left several messages on my cell phone that night after walking the property. He said he offered us $200,000 for the land and that's $30,000 more than you gave us."

"I still don't understand what you're saying" said Roy.

"I think you do understand what we're saying Roy. The reason we didn't get those fuckin' messages is because our cell phone was missing. You must have found out that Fredy was going to offer us more money so you stole our phone when you stopped by the hotel that night to give us the advance. We were fucked up so you could have easily taken it without us noticing."

Roy was shocked. He rolled his eyes and then looked squarely at Frank before responding.

"That's bullshit. I didn't take your God Damn phone and I didn't know about Fredy's offer until you told me about it just now. I made a legitimate business transaction after you both agreed to the offer I made. I don't know where you came up with this business about me stealing your phone, but my guess is that you concocted this story in a feeble attempt to get more money. If your phone is really missing, I would venture to say that one of you assholes lost it when you were wasted. I've never taken anything from anybody in my entire life, and I'm sure Eric Fredy would tell you the same. As far as I'm concerned, you two are a couple of the poorest excuses of human beings that I've ever met. Your grandfather willed this land to you and your only worry was to get as much money as possible for it, and then to get the hell out of here as quickly as possible. I'd bet my life that you didn't even have the decency to visit his grave, and I would also bet that you've spent most of the money already."

Roy was feeling violently angry as he stepped towards the Richards' brothers.

"Now I'm going to tell you something that's factual. If you ever approach me again or step foot on this property I'll beat the living hell out of you both."

Frank and Brett looked at one another before Brett finally responded.

"How about we make a compromise, you give us $20,000 and we'll leave and never bother you again?"

As soon as the last word came out of Brett's mouth Roy busted open with a sarcastic laugh. He became silent a moment later and took two steps to line himself closely with Brett. Roy was about to lose his cool. The problems of his marriage had caused him to be hopelessly frustrated, and the ridiculous situation at hand was about to provoke him beyond control.

"Did you hear what I just said? I didn't take your phone! You know what, let's settle this right now" Roy shouted hatefully as he stripped off his flannel shirt.

"Let's go you useless mother fuckers!"

Brett Richards was about six feet tall but his build was lacking any sort of intimidating features. He stood there looking less and less confident as Roy stared him down. He said nothing and broke eye contact soon after. Roy swiveled his head forty-five degrees to concentrate on Frank, who had a fairly sizable build. Roy remembered how much both men had struggled during their walk over the land months before, they were breathing heavily because of their addiction to cigarettes, marijuana, and other drugs. Roy was certain their short windedness would cause them to lose a scrap against someone who simply refused to give up. Roy continued to stare at Frank Richards, waiting for him to make the first move. But after several more seconds passed, Frank also broke eye contact before moving towards the Ford Explorer. Brett followed him to the vehicle and then turned to face Roy with one hand on the passenger side door handle.

"You screwed us man, I know you took that phone. This is not over."

Instead of responding to the additional accusation, Roy turned with a sigh of relief. His anger had settled as he thought about how his behavior would not be a good example for his children, had they been there watching him. Also, he was getting a bit old to challenge a pair to a scrap even if they were a couple of idiots. Brett and Frank Richards held their hands out of the window with extended middle fingers as they drove away. Roy did the same with his right hand and waved with his left, sporting a smile like that of an angel. He doubted that he would have to speak to them again.

Gage was somewhat concerned after Roy finished telling him about the encounter with the Richards' that morning.

"Maybe you should call the police Roy."

"I'm not worried about them Gage, there just a couple of greedy idiots who want more money for drugs. But you're probably right, I will call the police if I see them again."

Chapter Ten

November 14th, 1995, brought an expected rise in the temporary population of the Upper Peninsula. Thousands of people traveled over the Mackinac Bridge and through Menominee, Iron Mountain, and Ironwood to seek out hunting areas. A portion of native Yooper's despised the northern migration of the "tourists," who crowded areas that were very quiet and peaceful during the other 350 days of the year. Deer camps that had not been tended to for most of the year were now filled with heat, hunters, and good cheer for which any person would enjoy. Sportsmen and women who did not own property set up campers or tents on the never ending expanses of state, corporate, and federal land, and others would choose the much easier option of lodging at hotels. Local business owners of all kinds applauded the onset of deer season because the summer season and associated tourist boom was now a memory. Hunters bolstered the profits of gas stations, grocery stores, and sport shops while purchasing supplies for themselves and their camps.

A celebration was underway at the Gustafson camp south of Ishpeming. The eight beds would be filled by men of various beliefs and backgrounds, some of whom resided in Ishpeming and others who were forced to leave to find work elsewhere. Cousins Keith and Jack Gustafson lived in Colorado and Texas, and they were the most excited to be at the camp because they were only able to visit their home for a week during deer season and another during the 4th of July. Keith had graduated from

NMU with a bachelor's degree in Industrial technology and also received a Master's degree in Business Administration from the University of California before finding an excellent job in Colorado Springs. Jack Gustafson had moved to Texas at the age of twenty-one and had worked for a beef processing plant ever since. Both men had married and were currently raising two children each. The remainder of the hunters consisted of a miner, a teacher, a retired mine manager, a retired contractor, a logger, and a student. The group got along very well although at least one spirited debate would take place every day. These debates were normally in regards to politics, unions, and most often the almighty Whitetail deer. After all, deer were the reason the men gathered here each and every year after battling daily challenges that life imposed upon them. The camp was a brief vacation from reality which allowed the individual to enjoy the company of others, and to also reflect on their current situation while spending countless hours in a deer blind or walking alone. Some of the "blinds," sometimes referred to as "stands," consisted of small shacks equipped with a heater but most were just an old chair surrounded by conifer boughs for camouflage. Most used corn, apples, and carrots to attract the deer within view in hopes that at least one would have the ivory white antlers that all hunters dreamed of. There was not an abundant amount of deer in the north central U.P., especially after the winter of 1994 which caused one half of the population to perish from above average snow accumulation and below average temperatures.

Expectations among the hunters were minimal after Gage and Roy reported that only a few scrapes and rubs were found while scouting their property and the surrounding public land before the season. But even so, everyone was in great spirits fueled by cheap beer and whiskey, humorous jokes, and entertaining stories. Gage's sick sense of humor was at its peak during deer season and most of the practical jokes he played on his fellow camp members involved the "outhouse". The outhouse was a small 4 foot by 4 foot building constructed over a hole with a toilet seat included. Some property owners had outhouses that were more extravagant than others, and a few relied merely on a wooden chair with a hole cut through the seat. Gage loved to play tricks on his friend Don, who was often called a "cheese head" because he resided in Wisconsin. On one occasion, Gage placed a handful of crushed laxatives in Don's chile and then watched him squirm around and moan after supper until he bolted for the outhouse. Gage and his cousin John then snuck up on the outhouse with a video camera while Don was squealing loudly inside. The door was flung open and John began to record helpless Don on a camcorder, as he sat there red faced and sweaty. Don was unable to move with his pants around his ankles. He reached for a spare toilet seat from the floor to use as a shield as Gage pelted him with dozens of snowballs. Don could only threaten and cuss at them as they recorded the comedy scene with the camera. They submitted the tape to *America's Funniest Home Videos,* hoping to win the $100,000 grand prize, but hadn't received a response. The producers must have thought it was too gruesome.

Wolf tracks were discovered by Gage and Roy during that week which excited Gage immensely. Gray wolves were extirpated from Michigan in the early 1900's but had begun to recolonize the Upper Peninsula slowly, dispersing from a source population in Minnesota. The Wildlife Biologist in Gage touted the ongoing recovery of wolves but his father was not the least bit enthused about it.

"Wolves are deer killers Gage. We got rid of them once and now here they are again. If they recover in the U.P. we'll see how your deer hunting is ten years from now, Mr. Biologist."

"Gosh dad, severe winters kill a hell of a lot more deer than wolves and other predators in the U.P."

"Says who Gage?"

"Says the research dad. The Department of Natural Resources has proven, through research, that the primary limiting factor for deer is winter snow depth. Many deer die from malnutrition and starvation when snow depths are excessive late in the winter due to a rise in their metabolism."

"Bullshit Gage. Many deer are killed during the winter when they are ambushed in deep snow by wolves, coyotes and bobcat."

"Dad, do you even know the difference between additive and compensatory mortality of deer?"

"Fuck the DNR."

"What?" said Gage.

"I'm not talking about this anymore, you've been brain washed Gage."

"Dad, I studied this at NMU and….."

"Fuck NMU!" exclaimed John from his chair by the wood stove, followed by a deep and annoying laugh.

Gage shook his head in disgust and walked towards the sauna while Roy and the other camp members chuckled with great enjoyment.

By November 23rd, two bucks were hanging from the buck pole and most of the hunters had returned to their families and homes. Gage attended most of his classes throughout the season but was able to enjoy the nightlife and slept at the camp on most nights. The camp hosted only a handful of hunters during the second week of deer season but many fellow hunters from other camps came to visit during that time. Gage, like his father and brother, immensely enjoyed walking during the last few days of the hunting season. A fresh track could be found in any nearby swamp and slowly followed until the animal circled around or stopped to get a look at its follower. The pursuit was always quite exciting, but the tracker would very seldom get a good look at the deer because of the thick conifers between he and the animal.

Gage was also obsessed with the prospect of buying more land and was very pleased that his brother was able to do so through his business. Roy and Gage would sometimes travel to these properties near the end of deer season to hunt a different area. Before returning to town on the last day of deer season, the remaining hunters "broke" camp, which entailed draining the sauna and pumps, cleaning the camp, and removing all of the perishable foods. The atmosphere in the camp on that last day of the season was similar to that of a funeral. Gage, John, Roy, and Robert Gustafson moped around doing the chores while wishing the season could continue for just a few more days. Most hunters experience a post deer season depression that consumes them until mid-December, and finally the Christmas Holiday spirit arrives and uplifts them once again.

Although Gage was saddened by the close of deer season, he could not afford to take his mind off of school. He had slacked a bit during November but now it was necessary for him to put forth his greatest effort to finish the semester on a positive note. The final exams were quickly approaching and he studied more intensely than ever to prepare himself. Unlike the semester when he began to stumble and eventually drop out, Gage actually enjoyed his classes and looked forward to learning everything possible about the business of business.

He finished the semester with a 3.5 grade point average which caused his mother to drop a dozen eggs on the floor when he told her.

"Oh my goodness, congratulations Gage!"

She followed up with a shower of hugs to show her son how proud she was. Gage was already one third done with remaining college courses with only two more semesters to go. He took advantage of the semester break by working as many hours as possible.

During the evenings he rented movies and visited his family, spending much time with his niece and nephew over the Christmas holidays. He was addicted to Khora and Otto and began to think more about his own future possibilities of becoming a father. Gage understood that he would have to get over his fear of women and marriage if he wanted this to happen. He continued to have a sour taste for relationships due to the break up with Sherri Anderson, but did not feel the hate for her that plagued him before. He began to contemplate whether he might call her in a few weeks.

On December 31st, Gage decided to call his friends in the Ishpeming area to celebrate the arrival of 1996. Gage predicted that 1996 would be one of the best years of his life; he would graduate in August and hopefully find a good job shortly thereafter. The classes he enrolled in for the winter semester sounded even more interesting than those he took during the fall, but Gage knew they would be more difficult. He piled up on classes with a total of nineteen credits to ensure he would graduate on time. Gage fully intended to put in the time necessary to do well in each of his classes and would cut down his hours at the warehouse if need be.

Gage was pleased when Dave and four other friends returned his calls and decided to join him for an evening at Jack's Tee Pee Bar, a popular establishment in downtown Ishpeming. New Year's Eve and the 4th of July were two nights throughout the year when a person could visit the bar and be sure to see many friends from high school that had since left the area. Most Ishpeming natives returned to their beloved home to spend time with family and friends during these holidays. His friends were waiting for Gage when he arrived shortly after 8:00 p.m. They sat together at a table near the window and Dave ordered two pitchers of cold beer to kick things off.

After an hour of heavy drinking and conversations regarding work, college and other topics of responsibility, a group of young ladies entered the bar which prompted Gage to interrupt his own sentence with an "Oh my". He recognized most of them from high school as they had graduated two or three years after he did. They no longer looked like high schoolers however, but rather mature college students equipped with bodies that symbolized perfection. The six young men that spoke of only topics that would have pleased their mothers had now transformed into sex seekers whom any young woman's father would dread. The young ladies were all dressed very well, wearing snug blue jeans and tight shirts or sweaters. Two familiar feelings overtook Gage almost instantaneously; the alcohol had provoked the onset of a welcomed buzz and the entrance of the girls caused him to recall the desire of sexual intercourse. Gage didn't think about sex constantly as most men of his age did, but had moved his recent priorities to the back of his mind to make room for other short term possibilities. Gage was not interested in a relationship that would take more than a few hours of his time, especially after being side casted by Sherri Anderson long before. His mind set was similar to a white tailed buck in rut whose only immediate purpose was to breed any attractive female that would have him. Gage promised himself that he would not be too fussy, he would go above and beyond the call of duty to get himself laid that night.

The bar was filling quickly as Gage and his friends discussed their options over a mug of beer and a shot of Hartley's brandy, each of them knowing from experience that only one out of the six would find himself alone with a temptress later that night. One out of six at best. And that one person would more than likely be Chris Clark. He was the first to leave the table, like a single wolf breaking away from the pack. Chris had always relied on perseverance as his most equitable talent, and he made it clear to his friends that there was no place for self-consciousness when one is searching for a mate. Gage had witnessed this on many occasions during high school and afterward. At the beginning of his courting ritual, Chris was known to approach the most attractive women and then move on to the hefty ones as his level of intoxication grew in parallel with the number of rejections inflicted. Chris had always declared that his time tested method would usually lead to success, as documented in his "screwing diary", which was updated after each night on the town. Chris did admit that he sometimes woke up next to a partner that more resembled a gorilla than a beauty queen but insisted Gage would be satisfied with his method if he put forward the necessary effort. Gage's problem, however, was that no matter how drunk he became he was usually not able to build enough boldness to approach an attractive female. Nor did he consider himself the outgoing type which normally left him speechless even when he was approached. Such an unfortunate occurrence had taken place shortly after Gage returned to college while he was studying in a hallway of the Seaborg Center at NMU. He was taken by surprise when a gorgeous blonde sat next to him and attempted to strike a conversation. For no explainable reason other than that she was simply hitting on him, she introduced herself and described some of the classes she was taking. Gage was so intimidated by her beauty that he was having a very hard time coming up with anything to say. But finally, after she paused for a second time and waited for Gage to speak, he opened his mouth to ask her if she would like to join him for a cup of coffee. But it was a mistake, a very, very big mistake. As he stared into her breathtaking green eyes, he became hypnotized and had forgotten about the tobacco in his mouth. When he finally built the courage to ask her out, he opened his mouth and snuff juice dribbled down his lip and onto his shirt. Gage tried to regain his composure but it was far too late. She had already stood up and walked away with a grimace on her face.

"Son of a bitch" he said quietly as he watched her walk out of sight.

Gage decided to tell the embarrassing story to his friends at the table that night and they laughed for a very long time.

"Tonight will be a different story!" Gage exclaimed as he stood up to move himself closer to the group of prospects. The girls had situated themselves at the other end of the bar and Gage planned to slowly work his way in that direction while greeting other familiar faces on the way. He was impressed by the self-confidence he was feeling which was partially fueled by beer but mostly by other factors. Gage was doing well in school, he was now very much independent, and he had been working out quite a bit to keep himself in shape. He was a good looking young man with blonde hair and dark brown eyes, an impressive build, and most importantly a genuine personality. He was much like his brother in that he was a very likeable person who usually put others before himself. But tonight he wanted to put himself first. Tonight he didn't want to be a good person; he would get drunk and hopefully find a woman to share a one night stand with. His apartment had been cleaned that day and new sheets were placed on his bed in preparation. He had even purchased a fancy candle in confident anticipation of the event.

Gage was in fine shape, enjoying himself very much while carrying on conversations with a number of friends that he had not seen in quite some time. He noticed that Chris had already approached the attractive group of women, so this allowed him the opportunity to follow suit. Gage walked up with a beer held in one hand and the other in his pocket. Even though he was somewhat intoxicated, the shyness set in anyway and he just stood there looking at Chris, unable to make eye contact with any of the young ladies. After a few minutes of listening to Chris make an ass of himself, Gage felt comfortable enough to smile at whoever caught his eye. He turned to find an acquaintance standing right next to him. It was Josie Strong and she had also attended school in Ishpeming a few years after Gage, but he hadn't recognized her when she entered the bar with the others.

"Hi Gage" she said with a stunning smile. Josie Strong had grown up in the same neighborhood as Gage so he knew her well as a childhood friend, from the days of playing games such as high chase and kick the can. But because they were separated by a year and Josie was the academic type in high school and Gage was not, they didn't interact very often after middle school. But now Gage couldn't take his eyes off her. In addition to her bright smile, Josie had large hazel green eyes and beautiful auburn red hair arranged neatly into a flowing pony tail. Gage liked pony tails.

"Hi Josie, I've not seen you in a long time. How are you?"

Because Gage knew Josie at least somewhat, he didn't feel the usual nervousness associated with talking to a female and he settled into a very long conversation with her. Josie explained that she had been accepted to the University of Minnesota after graduation from Ishpeming and was currently in her senior year as an education student. She chose the University of Minnesota because her older brother and sister lived nearby and therefore Josie was able to spend her free time with their families. Her grand plan was to graduate from college in the spring of 1996 and then move back to the central Upper Peninsula to do her student teaching. Her parents still lived in Ishpeming and she told Gage that this was the main reason she wanted to move back. She went on to inform him that she hoped to be married with three children, a horse, and a nice home outside of town; all by the age of twenty eight. Gage was baffled by her precise explanation of what was to come and he then realized that he had similar projections for a life with Sherri Anderson before she betrayed him. Gage was not one to confide in anyone except his mother but for some unknown reason he suddenly became an instant mouthpiece in the presence of Josie Strong. He opened himself up to her by revealing his life's story and even embellished upon the sudden halt of his relationship with Sherri. Gage went on to describe his plans of graduating after the summer semester of 1996 and his career goals of becoming a successful financial analyst afterward. Gage didn't want to come across as the easily domesticated type so he didn't speak about marriage or having children, but he did convey the strong feelings he felt for his niece and nephew. This was enough to make her smile once again. Gage wasn't bashful about his feelings for horses either; he absolutely hated them. He told Josie a comical story about a long awaited horse ride that he took at the age of sixteen which resulted in him being bucked off, and the subsequent demolition of his brand new cowboy hat. Gage refused to ride or go anywhere near horses after that day, he was deathly afraid of them.

Gage and Josie continued to talk about a number of different things that they were both interested in and began to exchange gentle touches after spending ninety minutes together. They laughed as they relived stories as close childhood friends. Gage felt a very strong connection to Josie and he was certain that she did too. It was almost like a dream, except in this dream there was no way in hell that Gage Gustafson was having sex on New Year's Eve. It was apparent to him that she was not that type, but he didn't much care about that after spending a portion of the evening with her. He now felt more like the man he truly was rather than a horny dog like his friend Chris. After Josie was torn away by one of her friends, Gage just stood there for awhile thinking about what had just happened.

The bar was packed as the year 1996 approached, and several people moved between Gage and Josie as they scrambled to the rail to order more drinks. They exchanged glances periodically but Gage finally decided that it would not be proper to fight through the crowd to reunite himself with her, so he turned away to find his friends instead. His buddy Chris was hard at work only a few feet away. He was noticeably drunk and tactlessly trying to convince one of Josie's friends to leave the bar with him. Gage watched and listened as Chris made one final ill attempt to court the attractive brunette. "Sweetheart, I'm gonna make love to you tonight one way or another, so you might as well be there" he said.

Gage was in the midst of taking a swig of beer when he heard Chris's words tumble out over his drunken tongue without any forethought. He had no choice but to spit the beer on the floor while choking back a laugh. The young lady slapped Chris hard enough to move the feather of his hair from right to left and Gage continued to laugh uncontrollably. Chris reassembled himself and fixed his hair while turning his attention to Gage.

"You know Gage, most guys would give up and go home right about now. But do you think I will? No Sir. I'll be pouring the coals to some chick in the back of my car by the time this bar closes, and you'll be sleeping in your apartment all alone."

Gage nodded in agreement and then walked back towards the bar to order one more beer. He looked for Josie but she was surrounded by a group of friends and other dogs just like Chris. Gage had never been an aggressive person so he did not feel inclined to push his way through a crowd to compete for her attention. Gage hoped otherwise but he began to think the meeting with Josie was nothing more than a friendly conversation with a very nice girl. After saying a brief hello to another friend, Gage looked up at the T.V. that was mounted above the bar. A celebration was well underway in New York City and a one minute count-down appeared on the screen. He felt a warm hand on his arm and he turned to see her standing there with those beautiful eyes looking at him once again. He was surprised and the nervousness set in as he unsuccessfully searched his mind for the appropriate words.

"I'm…..I'm glad you came back over" he said.

Gage noticed that she looked quite nervous now as well, her neck was blotchy with redness as she prepared to respond.

"Gage, I've never done this before but I've had a few glasses of wine. I probably won't see you again for a long time so I'm going to say this and then I'll leave you alone. I have had a crush on you for as long as I can remember. I still have your high school football pictures and it was me that used to call your parents' house and hang up when you answered the phone. You probably don't remember this but I took care of you one night when you were very drunk during your senior year. You had been in a fight at a party and I found you passed out in an alley by the neighbor's house. Do you remember?"

Gage was stunned.

"Ah, no. Sorry, I don't remember. But thank you. Thank you for doing that."

Josie laughed.

"You were in pretty rough shape and only had one shoe on and I walked you home, it was no problem at all."

Their conversation was interrupted by the loudness in the bar and they turned to the television to watch the ball drop. It was a perfect moment, Gage reached for her arm and gently pulled her closer. He moved in without hesitation and she met him halfway. The kiss lasted for only a few moments but it was the best one that Gage had ever taken part in. They held each other close while wishing a happy new year to one another. Josie gave Gage her phone number and asked him to call her in Minnesota.

"I hope you call me very soon Gage."

She left the bar an hour later after explaining that she had to drive back to Minnesota for work early the next day.

Gage held the phone number tightly in his hand as he walked towards the door shortly after Josie left with her friends; he was a happy man indeed. He bid farewell to each of his comrades as he passed them but then stopped just short of the door after seeing his pal Chris near the pool table. Chris had finally struck gold. He was making out with a fairly large girl sitting on the edge of the table. It was apparent that she was as drunk or even more so than Chris. The pair were attacking each other, drunken kisses so frantically exchanged that their lips were missing the others' more often than not. Gage laughed once again as he walked out the door.

"Perseverance pays" he mumbled to himself with a smirk.

Chapter Eleven

Gage met his family for dinner on New Year's Day and his mother immediately noticed his elevated mood. He gave her some of the details about Josie Strong the night before.

"She sounds like a nice girl Gage, and she comes from a very nice family too."

Gage's father said what he always did whenever he overheard any conversation about the beginnings of relationships.

"I didn't get married until I was 32 years old. There's no time for women if you want to be in the woods."

"Oh, don't be so positive Robert," Sarah exclaimed sarcastically.

Roy and Kaylie arrived with the kids shortly after and Kaylie was in one of her usual depressing moods. Gage could barely stand to be around her and he could not understand how his brother put up with it. After dinner, Gage offered to take the children sledding at the nearby playgrounds and Kaylie quickly accepted. The temperature was twenty-nine degrees which was rare for the Upper Peninsula during the brutal month of January, so Gage thought it would be a good day to spend some time outside. He and the kids had a great time although little Otto fell out of his sleigh and hurt himself twice. As they walked back to the house Gage sensed that something was bothering Khora.

"What's wrong Khora?"

The six year-old looked up to her Uncle with a concerned expression.

"Uncle Gage, why do my mommy and daddy fight so much?

They yell at each other almost every night when daddy gets home cause he doesn't want mommy to go bowling."

Gage was saddened that a six year old was exposed to such arguing; she was much too young to be worried about her parents' problems.

"All moms and dads argue just like sisters and brothers do Khora."

"But my mom is never happy with my dad Uncle Gage."

"It'll get better Khora" said Gage.

Later that evening, Gage made plans with his dad and brother to spend the following weekend at the deer camp for a rabbit hunting trip. It would be the last weekend of Gage's semester break before he returned to school. A relaxing weekend at his most favorite place in the world would be a nice treat, a calm before the pressure of nineteen credits overwhelmed him. Gage was very excited to return to NMU but he was slightly worried about the amount of work he had taken on. If he did not complete the winter semester with satisfactory grades he would not be able to graduate in August. He would then be forced to enroll for another semester in the fall of 1996; this would postpone his dream of becoming a financial advisor. No matter what it took, Gage swore to himself that he would not allow for that unfortunate possibility.

Gage waited until Thursday to call Josie Strong even though he would have liked to do so on Monday. She was not in so he left a message with her brother. Gage put in fifty- five hours at the warehouse that week in a final attempt to pocket enough money for supplemental spending cash throughout the winter semester. Because his course workload would be so demanding, Gage decided not to work at the warehouse any longer. He would continue the sixteen hour shifts at the Rainbow Bar on most Saturdays which would be difficult enough.

So after his last morning shift at the warehouse on Friday, Gage bid farewell to the employees and thanked Mike Tasson before driving to his parent's house. There he met his dad, Roy, and his cousin John and they all piled into Roy's truck. Gage sat in the back seat with John and a big hound named Hort. Hort was John's dog, a Black and Tan that could "drive" rabbits like no other dog the men had ever seen. He weighed about seventy pounds and had an outstanding nose for the snowshoe hare and long legs that proved to be an asset in deep snow.

They drove south from town on County Road 581 and then headed west on the Island Lake Road. Because the access road to the deer camp was not drivable due to deep snow, they walked into the camp from the east using snowshoes. Hort was attached to a leash so that he would not disappear on a fresh track while the group traveled two miles west to the camp. The conditions were perfect. The temperature was in the low twenties which would allow Hort to easily smell the rabbits, and a mild system had deposited two inches of fresh snow the night before. The sun was shining and all of the four men were in a pleasant mood. They wore backpacks with clothes and food inside, and each carried a shotgun across their breast.

Much work was necessary at the camp when they arrived. The camp and sauna stoves were lit, snow was melted to prime the pumps, and the roof was shoveled off to ensure that it would not collapse as there was a great deal of snow yet to come before the arrival of spring. Robert Gustafson always demanded that all chores be completed before any hunting was done and the boys knew better than to argue with him. The work was done within an hour and the camp was partially heated, so Robert gave the go ahead to cut the dog loose. Hort was going crazy after being tied to a tree for nearly an hour, tortured by the scent of fresh rabbit tracks in the camp yard. After Gage's dad directed Roy and John to their usual positions near the swamp, he grabbed his gun with a smile and began to walk down an old logging road. Gage knew what to do. He would wait until his dad yelled across the swamp to Roy and John after he was in place, and then Gage would release the dog from his bothersome leash. Gage watched his father stride away flawlessly on snowshoes, quite impressive for a sixty-six year old man.

Gage took a moment to thank God for his father's health, he knew of many older men that could no longer hunt and fish because of their declining body condition. Many of whom stayed indoors watching television for most of any given day, biding their time until their lives were over. Gage found himself praying several times per week since re-enrolling at NMU, and he was certain that it helped him to live as a better and more responsible individual.

Gage was trying his best to console the poor hound while waiting for his father to yell, but old Hort was nearly strangling himself by putting his weight toward the fresh track at the end of his leash. Finally he heard his dad yell "ok lad, let that crazy bastard go free." Gage used most of his strength to pull the dog back to allow enough slack to unbuckle the strap and then off he went.

"He's in the swamp" yelled Gage and soon after any living organism within one square mile could hear the bellow of the hound. Hort was already on a rabbit and Gage closed his eyes for a moment to enjoy the deep voice of the Black and Tan. Meanwhile and from different corners of the swamp, Roy, John, and Robert Gustafson closed their own eyes for a moment as well. Gage listened for a few minutes until he determined which way the dog was headed and then began to walk in the opposite direction of his father. The snowshoe hare was taking Hort in a large circle as rabbits often do, and each of the men would be most likely positioned for a shot on its' route. It was typical of Hort to move very fast in pursuit until he tired somewhat, so the rabbit also moved fast which made for a difficult shot. Gage walked slowly for fifty yards and then stopped when he heard the dog turn his way. A shot was fired followed by a "son of a bitch" from his cousin John, who was well known for shooting too often with very little success. Another blast from a 20 gauge shotgun interrupted the dog's harmony.

"Shit, I missed him" yelled Roy.

With a broad smile on his face, Gage waited for Hort to resume his howl. When Hort found the scent once again Gage dropped quietly onto one knee and partially raised his gun in anticipation. It was his turn and he was fully aware that bragging rights would be acquired if he got the rabbit after his cousin and brother missed.

The snowshoe hare, commonly referred to as a rabbit, was no stranger to being a hopeful meal for numerous predators on a daily basis. Coyotes, fishers, martens and owls were only a fraction of the animals that depended on rabbits as a primary food source. It was an absolute miracle that they were able to survive and proliferate in such a harsh environment. But they did, and there were always good numbers of rabbits in the spruce swamp near the Gustafson camp.

Gage could see a glimpse of Hort every few seconds and he knew the rabbit was in front of him so he prepared for a shot. The stock of the gun was raised against his right shoulder and the barrel was rested on his left hand. And then from the corner of his eye he saw movement to his right side and the gun was swiveled across for a shot. The rabbit had almost passed him by because its' white fur blended well with the surrounding snow. Gage blasted three times in rapid succession as the rabbit darted through tag alders and behind sphagnum moss hummocks before disappearing further into the swamp. He walked over to where he thought the rabbit was, hoping to find the animal laying quietly on the forest floor. Hort showed up a few minutes later and trotted by Gage with his nose to the ground, confirming that he had missed the target.

"You're pushing that rabbit too fast Hort" Gage yelled in an attempt to blame the dog rather than himself.

John and Roy's chuckles echoed below the snow covered trees and Gage raised his middle finger even though they were too far away to see him. All three of the unsuccessful shooters knew that Robert Gustafson was not likely to miss the rabbit and it was headed directly his way. The dog began to howl once again and a single shot was fired soon after. The swamp became briefly silent once again.

"That a boy Hort, good dog. You boys don't need to use those fucking pump shotguns, you just have to learn to make one good shot" yelled Robert from across the swamp.

By the end of the day, eight snowshoe hares had been harvested after seventeen shots were fired. It was a very successful hunt. The men enjoyed a meal of venison for supper and gave all of the remaining meat to Hort as a token of appreciation. He laid on the couch all night while each of the hunters took turns petting him and feeding him snacks. Good rabbit dogs live like kings in the Upper Peninsula of Michigan.

Roy had a carefree attitude, he was laughing a lot and seemed to be enjoying himself a great deal while playing cards and taking saunas. Gage was happy to see his brother in such fine spirits and although he hoped that things had suddenly improved with Kaylie, chances were they had not. Roy didn't bring up the issues with his wife so Gage didn't either. When he did, Gage planned to tell Roy about the concerns his daughter expressed after sledding the weekend before.

Even though all were tired from the fresh air and from walking on snowshoes, they stayed up late drinking cheap whiskey and playing cards. Robert was in rare form. He told stories about dead brothers, uncles, and grandfathers who fished and hunted the same areas the family did presently. He danced with a broom after winning four straight card games and then went off to bed at midnight. Roy, Gage, and John all knew Robert Gustafson lived for days like this; days of togetherness in the woods with his sons and nephew.

Chapter Twelve

Gage returned from camp in the early afternoon of Sunday, January 9th. He had two very important issues on his mind as he entered the apartment and walked directly to the phone. Gage had not mentioned Josie Strong during the rabbit hunting trip, but his thoughts were totally consumed by the memory of her on New Year's Eve. There were three messages on the answering machine but none of them were left by her. Gage was very disappointed that she had not returned the call and his cautious side immediately took over. He had assumed that she would have left a message for him and then he would call her again that evening. A feeling of doubt overcame Gage and he decided not to call Josie that night, he would wait for her to call him instead. Maybe she was a bit drunk at the bar and later regretted giving her phone number to him. Gage hadn't asked her if she had a boyfriend, maybe she did and had second thoughts when she returned to Minnesota. Gage sat down at his kitchen table to pick apart his pleasant recollection of Josie Strong. It was a defensive mechanism used to protect himself, created after the breakup with Sherri Anderson. After all, he barely knew Josie. There was no justifiable reason for him to think so highly of her after such a brief visit in a bar. Gage used to believe that Sherri Anderson was nearly perfect but in hindsight he knew that she was a poor excuse for a girlfriend. Josie had revealed that she had a crush on him for a long time, but Gage now dismissed the statement as nonsense provoked by a few glasses of wine. Why would she wait for several years to inform him of this attraction?

It was now all bullshit in Gage's mind, and he decided that he would not worry about it anymore. The last thing he needed right now was a bothersome distraction. Gage would begin his winter semester classes on the following day and he convinced himself that school would be his only priority until he graduated after the following summer.

He arranged and labeled notebooks for each class and stocked his backpack with supplies that were necessary for daily responsibilities. He organized himself by writing down a schedule that spoke for almost every minute of his time throughout the day. It began with his 8:00 a.m. class and ended at 11:00 p.m. after exercising for forty- five minutes. There would be very little time available for television, rabbit hunting or ice fishing throughout the remainder of the winter. He planned to visit his niece and nephew twice a week if he felt comfortable with his work load at school.

The next day was a busy one. Gage attended his classes which were stacked one after the next from 8:00 a.m. until 1:00 p.m., and then ran over to the University store to purchase the necessary books as required by the instructors. The cost of the books stunned Gage as he wrote a check for $240. He figured the tuition costs were high enough that the University should not need to inflate the price of books so much. He would be lucky to get $100 when he sold the books back to the store after the semester ended, a typical example of customer gouging. Gage was now much more conscious of the money spent because it would have to be repaid after graduation. He was home by 4:00 p.m. that afternoon and gobbled down two bowls of his mom's chile before settling in to study.

He began to read the first chapter of a book titled *Professional Finance* and was immediately taken in by the content. From this book and daily lectures, Gage would learn much more about interest rates and the inverse effects they inflict on bonds, the fundamentals of banking, the mortgage process, and much more. Gage was not interested as much in banking finance as he was in the general stock market, but he vowed to do very well in all of his classes because the information learned would prove to be an asset at one time or another. He was certain that he could conquer the nineteen credit course load if he studied relentlessly on each night other than Saturday. He enjoyed bartending for the sixteen hour shift on Saturday and hoped that he could continue to do so through the winter and following summer. A group of fine looking women visited the bar each Saturday, and when Gage inquired about why they visited so often he found out that they came just to lay their eyes on him. He was a handsome young man no doubt, with broad shoulders and notable biceps. These features and a likable personality ensured a surprising amount of tips each weekend. And he needed the money. He also was attracted to a few of the ladies that practically threw themselves at him while visiting, but decided to resist until he was certain that Josie would not return the call.

Roy Gustafson had arrived home that evening in a very good mood. He was happy to see his children as always, and after greeting them he walked to the kitchen to say hello to his wife. He thought about her a lot over the weekend at camp and during that day as he cut timber. He had good news that he was sure would brighten Kaylie after he discussed it with her.

Very few people realized how successful Roy Gustafson had become. Because of his hard work and the hard work of his employees, the Gustafson Land and Log Company was doing better than ever. The business had expanded significantly as his good reputation spread across the area. Many private landowners contacted him on a weekly basis to harvest the wood on their property, and the large paper companies offered him as much work as he could take on. Roy didn't advertise his company but it was a well-known fact that he paid fair prices to the landowner for stumpage while harvesting the trees in a sustainable manner. Roy's company was a symbol of such ethics and this was the main reason he was sought after.

But an equally important reason for the success of his company was reliable and consistent production. After being hired, each employee was told they would do well as long as they worked very hard every day. Roy had to fire two individuals that allowed laziness to dominate their performance, but his present work force of fourteen men was unbeatable. Roy was certain that each man produced more wood than two average loggers working elsewhere, so he had no complaints about paying them what they were worth. He ran a tight ship but didn't interfere with anyone's job unless they asked, or unless they weren't pulling their weight. He was also a very understanding supervisor. An employee could be paid in advance if they were in a financial bind and each received three weeks of vacation in addition to sick leave. If unexpected profits were made, Roy would hand down a portion of those profits to the men in the form of a bonus. Roy respected his employees and they respected him in return. The men were split into three separate crews and would normally work on separate jobs that may be close in proximity or on opposite sides of the county. Roy now owned three processors and three skidders, of which could be operated by any of his men.

Roy would work with whatever crew needed him on that given day, but recently he had been devoting even more of his time to the acquisition or sale of vacant timberland. This was the second, and perhaps the most profitable component of the business. It required very little manpower, only a thoughtful mind and a feel for land and timber values. Roy had a knack for finding good deals on land and he spent at least ten hours per week scouring through classifieds and realtor publications. Most of the property he purchased had been acquired during the winter months when very few people were looking for land. After calling the realtor upon finding a recently listed parcel in a publication, Roy would walk through it on snowshoes and determine the value by assessing the timber. Sellers that did not want to hold the land until the following summer would normally let it go for a price that was significantly less than it was listed for. Roy would either sell the land during the following tourist season and use the profit to buy more, or he would keep it if the timber could be managed for a long term profit. Because he bought or sold land on almost a biweekly basis, he gave a great deal of business to the Ishpeming Community Bank because many short term loans were necessary throughout the course of the year. He made copies of interest statements that were paid in full and sent them to Brian Giroux at the National Savings Bank, his previous bank, just for spite. Roy held a grudge.

As a business owner Roy had one very serious fear; the fear of failure. Even though the company was doing extremely well, Roy knew there was an unlikely possibility that the company could fold if he was not able to find wood to cut or if timber and land prices plummeted. The monthly payments on six pieces of logging equipment were almost astronomical and these payments would continue to be made only if a great deal of wood was produced. Depending on the amount of monthly production, Roy would make additional principal payments on the loans to lessen the financial liability of the company. He refused to sell any of the productive forestland that had been acquired because it would prove to be a valuable asset if managed properly.

Roy was convinced that he could improve the relations with his wife. It was evident that Kaylie was not happy and it was his desire to change things for the better. They had two perfect children, a beautiful home, and a successful business, so there was no reason that happiness could not be associated with their personal lives. At least in Roy's mind. He knew the children were wearing Kaylie down and believed that she needed a secondary purpose in her life; a meaningful purpose that would give her a different type of responsibility which in turn would improve her demeanor. Roy intended to give her any option she desired to create an opportunity for change. He was a loving man and desperately wanted to make his wife a more loving woman and caring mother.

Roy hugged Kaylie, kissed her gently on the cheek, and asked her to sit down that night after work.

"Kaylie, I know you're not as happy as you were at one time

and I want to change that."

"What do you mean?" she asked.

"Well, I think you need to get out of the house more during the day. Our business is doing very well and we can now afford for me to work less. I've got excellent employees which sustains the business without me being there all the time. What I'm trying to say is that I can cut my hours down significantly, and I'll mostly just concentrate on real estate unless the guys need me."

Roy waited for Kaylie to respond. She looked at him with confusion.

"You'll be making less money if you do that won't you?"

"I might make less initially, but it's possible that I'll make more with less effort if I continue to find good deals on vacant land. This would allow me to stay home with the kids much more and would also provide you with the opportunity to either get an enjoyable job or go to college. We could find a good daycare provider to take care of the kids a couple days per week if needed. You can go to school for whatever you want Kaylie. I want you to be happy and I want you to be home with your family in the evenings. Right now you're miserable, we need to change that."

Kaylie started to cry uncontrollably as she hugged Roy. She regained her composure after a few minutes, stepped back, and looked at him with tears streaming down her face.

"Roy, I don't know if I'm capable of being a good wife and mother. I just don't know if it's in me."

Roy stepped towards her again and grabbed her shoulders with his strong hands.

"Don't say that Kaylie! This has been difficult because you were very young when Khora came along. You weren't able to work much or go to college before having children, but now is your chance. Now is the time for you to do something only for yourself, you can choose any career that appeals to you. We're going to make this marriage work Kaylie, no matter what."

Kaylie sat down at the kitchen table and wiped her tears away.

A few minutes passed, and then she got back up and put her arms around her husband.

"Yes. I think I can do this Roy. I want to go to college. This is what I need."

They embraced once again and then Roy ran to the phone to call his brother.

"Gage, you need to come over. Kaylie is going to enroll at NMU and we would like to look over your course booklet."

Gage knocked at the door within fifteen minutes, he was carrying the course booklet and pamphlets from various disciplines that he had saved. It was the happiest and most exciting evening that the Gustafson household had seen in quite some time. Kaylie and Roy looked over the endless possibilities of career paths and courses in the University catalog and Gage answered her questions about the requirements of liberal studies and other general questions about college as he played marbles with the kids. Gage was impressed by Kaylie's interest in college and a part of him believed that maybe she would be content after enrolling in classes. But a part of him also believed that Kaylie was anything but a decent person, no matter what Roy did for her. Her terrible upbringing had imposed a negative attitude upon her, but Roy hoped the opportunity to attend college would finally change her outlook.

After calling an advisor at Northern Michigan University the next morning, Kaylie Gustafson rushed out of the door at 8:15am while Roy graciously tended to the kids. If things worked out as she hoped, she would be able to enroll in a few classes if they were not already full. It was the second day of the winter semester so there was no time to waste. Her GED certificate and high school transcripts were brought to the admissions office and she was accepted to the University. Kaylie was warned that her acceptance was conditional upon receiving a 2.5 GPA, at the very least. The admissions officer politely informed her that she would be on probation for at least one year, and possibly longer depending on her grades. Three hours later Kaylie was enrolled in two 100 level classes; *Introduction to Computers* and *Introduction to Technical Writing*. Eight credits were enough for her first semester as a part-time student and fortunately those classes began on the second day rather than the first. She attended the classes that afternoon and immediately became interested in the lectures and atmosphere.

Kaylie Gustafson's life had changed in one day and she felt a new and exciting sense of independence. During her drive home that afternoon, she thought about which career she would choose. She thought about her children and wondered why she was so much more interested in herself than them. Kaylie did know one thing for sure; her love for Roy Gustafson had vanished long ago. She then realized that going to college would only worsen the situation with her husband by creating independence for her. Deep down, this is what she wanted. She wanted the freedom to enjoy her life for awhile without taking others into consideration, without the responsibilities of parenthood or marriage. She had been very content for a short time after marrying Roy and had since broken her addiction to drugs, but now the sense of satisfaction with her lifestyle had diminished beyond repair. Her duties as a mother felt more like an un-manageable burden than an enjoyable obligation. Kaylie felt that she had put a great deal of effort into becoming the woman that Roy wanted since they married, but now she accepted the fact that she was simply not suited for the job. She was not at all certain about where her new found passion for a career would take her, but she had enjoyed the atmosphere of the campus that day and would rely on fate to guide her. She also enjoyed the glances of the men that she passed by and sat next to in class. This is where she belonged, not at home raising children and cleaning a messy house. Kaylie Gustafson was turning out to be much like her own mother who had abandoned her at a very young age. She felt no remorse for her thoughts and her personality could not be changed by any man, not even by the love and dedication of Roy Gustafson.

Chapter Thirteen

On the following Sunday afternoon which concluded the first week of college courses, Gage Gustafson was enjoying a burger at Buck's Restaurant in Ishpeming. He had woken up just two hours before after working a sixteen hour shift at the Rainbow Bar. Saturday night had been much busier than expected because a large group of snowmobilers had arrived at 5:00 p.m. and stayed until closing time. Gage would have liked to think that it was his stunning personality and service that kept the tourists in the bar all evening, but he knew better. The usual small group of single, fine looking ladies teased the out-of-towners into buying drinks all night long. The girls had departed without warning at about 1:45am, leaving the snowmobilers with no one to escort them back to their hotel.

Gage made fifty dollars in tips that night and enjoyed a long conversation, although many times interrupted, with an executive from a mutual fund company. The fellow was with the group of tourists and was happily married, so he wasn't making an effort to court the females as his friends were. He sat at the bar for most of the evening and explained to Gage that he lived in Chicago but visited the Upper Peninsula at least twice every year. His name was Bill Meyers and he was the manager of a mutual fund offered by a company named Atlantic Financial. Because Bill Meyers seemed to enjoy talking about his education and career, Gage felt comfortable asking him a number of questions that would provide him with helpful knowledge in the future. Gage paid very close attention as Meyers explained how he arrived at his position with Atlantic Financial. He was a native to Marquette and had been a student at and graduated from Northern Michigan University with a degree in Finance. He worked for three years in the Lower Peninsula while obtaining his Master's degree from Central Michigan University. His apparent success was achieved not by using a special strategy but simply by working hard every day. He told Gage that the greatest asset that any working person could have is a solid personality and tactful approach. Meyers emphasized that such a personality consisted of a number of attributes, but most importantly the ability to interact positively with other people in a variety of situations.

"If you work hard and the people around you enjoy your company, you'll do very well. Some professionals have an ego problem because they figure they're smarter than others around them. Modesty is an underestimated characteristic. If you lead by example and portray your confidence in a modest way, people will revolve around you."

Meyers went on to explain that follow up is another very important part of a positive working environment.

"Make sure you always return phone calls as quickly as possible. People don't like to wait for answers to their questions. Their request may be a very low priority for you at that given time, but they will remember if you do not follow up in a timely manner. They need to feel important."

The advice given by Meyers was a valuable piece of information that Gage would store away for the future. He collected a business card from Meyers before he departed from the Rainbow bar that night.

As Gage continued to attack the delicious burger he noticed a vaguely familiar face on the other side of the restaurant. It was Emil Belland, a long time resident of Ishpeming who lived just a few doors down from Gage's parents'. Gage had fond memories of Emil from his childhood days, he was a gentle man who always said hello to the children of the neighborhood and allowed them to play football in his huge yard. He always offered a cold can of pop and other refreshments to the boys after the game was over. Emil was a bachelor who devoted his life to ski jumping, a once very popular sport that took place just east of Ishpeming at a hill known as "Suicide". Ski jumping was a treacherous sport and participants from all over the world travelled to Suicide Hill and the National Ski Hall of Fame in Ishpeming. Emil had been a national champion and Gage remembered watching him fly through the air like a bird as a young spectator. It seemed like yesterday. But now as Gage watched Emil attempt to stand up from the restaurant table, he realized how quickly time had passed. He recalled that his mother told him that Emil had a stroke recently, but it really didn't seem significant until now. The man that Gage remembered as an athlete now struggled to stand up from a table. He had retired in apparent good health from Cleveland Cliffs at the age of sixty, only to be partially paralyzed by a stroke shortly after. It wasn't fair for a healthy man to work so hard for so long, only to be denied his golden years after retirement. After approaching Emil and speaking to him for awhile Gage reminded himself to send a card to Emil, thanking him for being such a generous and caring person. It would be a nice thing to do and Emil would appreciate it. Gage was beginning to realize just how short one lifetime was.

Gage left the restaurant feeling even more determined to do well in school and to live well afterward. He stopped at his parents' house to see how they were doing, and then went back to his apartment for a long night of studying. He wrote out a well stated letter of appreciation on a card addressed to Emil Belland before beginning his school work.

By mid-April of 1996, Gage Gustafson was feeling somewhat burnt out from the endless hours of college courses and studying. His energetic attitude had now diminished to that of mere survival as the semester exams approached. He had just fought his way through a difficult month of course topics that were not nearly as appealing as those at the beginning of the semester, and so it was harder for him to retain the information. And one instructor in particular, Professor Weisinger, seemed to enjoy flunking as many students as possible. The exams he devised were designed to allow very few students to do well, and he did not grade on a curve. Gage hated him. In his opinion, Professor Weisinger was a terribly boring instructor who provided no insight as to what a student should concentrate on for exams. Instead of providing a stimulating learning environment, Weisinger concentrated on intimidation tactics and vague lectures that had caused almost half of the original attendees to drop out. Gage had done everything he could imagine to perform well on the tests but only had a "C" going into the final exam. If he did poorly on the final, he would not be able to graduate at the end of August as planned. Gage could not afford for this to happen. He even approached the unlikable Weisinger in his office months before, and asked him what more he could do to improve his grade. Weisinger was arrogant and acted like he had better things to do than converse with students.

"Perhaps you're not cut out for a career in Finance if you can't do well in my class."

"I disagree. No one does well in your class Professor Weisinger. Perhaps you're not cut out for a career as a professor" said Gage as he exited the office.

Gage felt good as the words came out of his mouth but in hindsight he knew it was a big mistake to insult a professor. The other remaining students felt the same about Weisinger; they talked about how happy everyone would be if he dropped dead. They would throw a party if it happened.

Gage had done very well in all of his other classes but those achievements only provided him with a partial sense of happiness. And that partial sense of happiness was short lived after a moment's thought about the upcoming exam in Weisinger's *Advanced Finance*

class. Gage devoted more of his time studying for that exam than all the others combined, and he became quite irritable in doing so. He was normally a quiet and patient person overall, but his family and friends noticed a lot of tension in his presence. He was also very frustrated that Josie Strong had not called him back and was angry at himself for not letting her memory be forgotten. He thought about her often and recalled the night they met on New Year's Eve. He tried to resign himself to admit that it was just too good to be true and would not allow himself to call her again.

The *Advanced Finance* exam was the last to be taken during the week of April 25th. Gage had already received the results of the other exams of which he had done very well. This boosted his confidence somewhat but he was still not able to sleep much the night before his exam with the hated Weisinger. The test was grueling and Gage used every minute of the two hour limit to answer and review the answers repeatedly. The grades were to be posted on the Professor's office door by 6:00 p.m. that evening, so Gage decided to stay on campus until then so his fate would be known before the weekend. He walked around the campus aimlessly for two hours and became less and less confident as time passed. His stomach had been in a knot for an entire week and he was fed up with worry. Gage began to think that Weisinger was right; maybe he wasn't cut out to be a financial planner after all. Maybe he should have stayed put at his previous job, he was very happy until the day that he met with that dammed Troy Morton who owned a finance business in Ishpeming. If he hadn't met with Morton to discuss his 401(k) he would probably be a salesman by now at Tasson Distributing. He would be making a better than average wage and might have already purchased a nice little house in Ishpeming. Instead, he had thrown himself into a pile of debt to return to college and had been pulling his hair out for four months trying to satisfy the relentless demands of the most unlikeable person he had ever known, Martin Weisinger.

Gage threw in a three finger pinch of snuff, which almost caused him to vomit after inhaling some of it, before walking into Jamrich Hall. He had now convinced himself that he flunked the exam, he reverted to immaturity and planned to piss all over Weisinger's desk if he was not there. Gage could not bear the thought of taking the class again and waiting to graduate until after the following fall semester, so he would instead return to the warehouse and beg for his job back. He walked down the stairs to the lower level of the building at a very brisk pace, sporting a "don't give a damn" expression. A small group of students were already gathered around the office as the professor taped the results onto his door. Weisinger passed by in the hallway and Gage projected an ice cold stare directly at him but was not even acknowledged.

A short line was formed and each of the other students exuded a noticeably nervous behavior as their turn approached. The atmosphere was eerily quiet. The first student's index finger was shaking as she moved it slowly down the list of names, and she broke into a hysteric sobbing episode when it stopped at her score; "40%." Gage began to shake when it was his turn also and he tried to open the office door before he looked for his grade. The door was locked, he would not be able to carry out his revenge on the desk of Martin Weisinger. Gage reminded himself of Rudy Rudiger as his finger scrolled down the list to find his name. He triple checked the number as a flabbergasted smile stretched from ear to ear;

"Gage Gustafson - 80% (top score)." Gage threw his arms into the air and screamed with joy as he ran out of the building and onto the campus lawn. He put his backpack down for a pillow and laid there for a few minutes, totally elated by the good news. In addition to receiving the highest score of all on the final, his overall grade would now be pushed up to a "B-". He was much more proud of the "B-" than the "A's" he had received in his other classes because he had worked so hard to earn it. Suddenly, Gage was now certain that he would become the most successful individual to ever graduate from Northern Michigan University with a degree in Finance. His doubts disappeared and his confidence returned. Gage was one step closer to capturing his dream.

Upon receiving the news from her son about a very successful semester at NMU, Sarah Gustafson invited him and the rest of the family over for supper to celebrate. She was quite tired from watching her grandchildren that day but was immediately energized by Gage's achievement. Khora and Otto loved to be at Grandma's house. She was now caring for them one day per week to help Kaylie and Roy with their new schedules. Sarah was sixty-one years old and even though she offered to take the children more often, Roy thought it might be too hard on her. He arranged for alternate day care as necessary. Two young kids were quite demanding and they tended to take advantage of their grandma because she was a bit of a pushover.

Sarah served her famous spaghetti and meatballs for supper on that special evening, and each of the adults enjoyed a glass of red wine with their meals. Robert carried out a long winded toast to congratulate Gage and Kaylie for having the courage and desire to return to school. He went on to explain, as he did frequently to make a point, that he had no such opportunity as a young man. Robert had a job waiting for him at the Cleveland Cliffs Mather A mine when he graduated from high school.

Kaylie Gustafson seemed to be in a very good mood that night also, she had not yet received the final grades for her classes but was confident that she did well. She had tentatively decided that her career of choice would be nursing. Gage had doubts about Kaylie as always, he would be surprised if she really did well in her classes. When she said she was going to become a nurse, he almost laughed out loud. Gage hoped that he would be proven wrong but he was relatively sure that no matter what his brother did for Kaylie, she would never be happy.

Chapter Fourteen

Even though Kaylie seemed to be a more pleasant person after enrolling at NMU, Roy noticed that she continued to ignore him and the children by and large. He had approached her once before to discuss the problem, but she dismissed his concern by explaining that she must concentrate on college. He let it go, until that night in late April after dinner at his mother's house. Roy knew first-hand what a loving home was all about because he grew up in one. Robert and Sarah were typical of most married couples, they had minor problems and Roy remembered them arguing from time to time. But there was always a very strong sense of love between them, and Roy knew that a sense of love was lacking in his own relationship. Things weren't right in his home and they had not improved after Kaylie enrolled in school as he hoped. In addition, his depression had caused sadness and hopelessness to return in recent months. The medication was not working as it had early on and he could not understand why.

Roy sat next to Kaylie on the couch after he tucked in the children for the night.

"Kaylie, I need to talk to you."

Kaylie expressed that she was uncomfortable by squirming about before responding to him.

"What is it Roy?"

He reached for her hand, hoping that she would reciprocate but she huddled her arms around herself in a defensive manner.

"What is it this time?" she asked.

"Kaylie, you are obviously happy about school but I've seen no improvement in your behavior towards the kids and me. It's like we don't exist anymore. I want to make this better but there's nothing more I can do without…"

"Stop Roy, just stop! I've heard this all before. I can't change the way I am. I don't think this is going to work Roy. I'm not happy here anymore."

Roy was shocked, he had no idea how bad it was.

"What, what do you mean Kaylie?" Roy asked with tears forming in his eyes. He could sense something terrible was about to be revealed. Kaylie began to cry as well.

"I want a divorce Roy. I've been seeing someone else."

She had finally built the courage to say it.

"I'm sorry Roy, I really am."

Roy placed his hands over his face and began to sob, it was the first time Kaylie had seen him cry. Even Kaylie had something inside her that vaguely resembled a conscious and she tried to touch Roy in an effort to console him. He pushed her hand away and stood up abruptly from the couch.

"Who is he?" Roy screamed. "I'll kill him….how could you do this to me Kaylie, how could you do this to our children?"

Kaylie was not crying anymore. She stared at the floor, refusing to answer his questions. Roy couldn't stand to be in her presence any longer, he rushed out the door and bailed into his truck. He sat there for a long time, crying uncontrollably, trying to decide where to go. When he saw her walk out onto the porch the vehicle was started and the tires squealed out of the driveway.

Roy drove to the only place where he knew he would be alone. He arrived at the deer camp twenty minutes later and stood outside for a very long time, paralyzed by betrayal. He continued to cry while hyperventilating, unable to gather himself because of the unbearable pain. The woman that he had fallen so deeply in love with had just conveyed that she loved him no longer, that she was having an affair. The affair was probably with a student at the University where Roy had prompted her to attend.

The thought of divorce had never once crossed his mind; he had been sure until now that everything would somehow be fine if he continued to love her unconditionally. Despite numerous flaws, Roy worshipped Kaylie. And now, without the children on his mind, he was feeling like his life was over. His mental illness, which had become more pronounced in recent months, intensified the pain beyond his ability to cope.

Gage's phone rang at 3:00 a.m., and he woke with a smile from a very pleasant dream that had taken him into the future. He was a stock broker on Wall Street. But he began to worry instantly when he looked at the clock.

"Hello." Kaylie was crying on the other end.

"Kaylie what's wrong? Are the kids alright?"

"Yes. They're fine. Your brother is gone." Gage could barely decipher what she was saying.

"What do you mean he's gone?"

Gage assumed that a fight was underway and that Roy had finally gotten pissed off. The tone in his voice was not cordial.

"Stop crying and tell me what's going on," he demanded.

"We're getting a divorce Gage. I can't do this anymore" she said in a drunken tone.

Gage knew that his brother would never instigate a discussion of divorce, Kaylie must have brought this on.

"What can't you do anymore Kaylie? Can't you handle being treated like a queen, can't you handle being the mother of two beautiful children? Where the fuck is my brother?"

"I don't know" she said before hanging up the phone.

Gage scrambled to find his clothes while deciding where his brother might be. He threw on his jacket and ran outside to the truck. He was very upset.

"That bitch" he grumbled as he turned the key and drove off.

After driving through town a couple of times hoping that he would find Roy doing the same, Gage headed south towards the camp, suspecting he might be there.

Roy was not in a sensible state of mind and his clinical depression had intensified beyond his ability to see any remaining joy. He had erased all of the positive aspects of his life including two wonderful children, and now only concentrated on eliminating the overwhelming mental pain that surged through his body. His arms shook wildly as he balanced the rifle in the opposite direction of the norm. The muzzle of the barrel was finally stabilized and Roy moved his right thumb towards the trigger as he stared off into nowhere. The air was filled with the call of spring peepers. He could not think about anything other than taking his own life, it was the only option available.

Roy's attention was diverted from the barrel of the gun by the distant noise of a vehicle splashing through the recently melted snow on the road. Soon he could see the headlights flickering through the conifer trees that aligned the winding dirt road. Roy could tell it was Gage's truck by the sound. He hustled the gun into the camp, not quite understanding what he had been about to do.

Roy did not want company. Being an extremely prideful person and unlike most others, he was not able to reach out for help from those he loved. No one knew that Roy had depression other than he and Dr. Pruett. He had coped with it for his entire adult life, somewhat successfully, through hard work and loving his children. But now he only felt hopelessness and was absolutely unable to manage the internal pain.

Gage's truck was covered in mud from speeding down the two track road. The door was opened before the vehicle was put into park, and he jumped out on a brisk walk. Gage was also a very prideful individual but now was not the time to be silent. Now was not the time to be a listener because he knew his brother would probably not want to talk about it. He approached feeling very uncomfortable. Roy was standing on the porch in front of the headlights.

"Roy, are you alright?"

"I'm fine Gage, how are you doing?"

It was typical of Roy to deflect any concern shown by others because he was a giver just like their mother. Gage knew full well that he would have to dig deep to get Roy talking.

"Kaylie just called me Roy."

Roy's eyes were swelled and damp and it became immediately apparent to Gage how much pain he was in.

"I don't want to talk right now Gage. I just need some time alone. Please go."

"It's really cold out here Roy. Let's go inside and start a fire."

Without waiting for a response from his brother Gage walked into the camp and lit the gas lights. He brought some kindling in from the sauna and started a fire in the cast iron stove. He watched the fire emerge and patiently waited for Roy to walk into the camp. He didn't want to push him too hard.

The spring peepers were chirping so loudly that they could be heard from inside the camp over the crackling of the fire. After waiting for fifteen minutes, Gage walked back out onto the porch. It was time to initiate a difficult conversation. Roy was now sitting down, staring off into the swamp and Gage seated himself next to him.

"You've always been here for me when I needed you Roy. Now it's my turn. Please talk to me about this."

Roy stood up to distance himself, he did not want to break down in front of his brother. "Please leave Gage, the best thing you can do for me is to just give me some time."

The tone of Roy's voice was not one that conveyed a request but rather a demand. Gage had last heard that tone at the Rainbow bar, when Roy told him that he was going to take him home.

"I'm not leaving Roy, not until we talk about this. You'll feel better if you just tell me…"

"I don't want to talk to you!" Roy yelled as he reached down to grab Gage by his jacket.

"Now get the hell out of here."

He lunged Gage off the porch and backed him up towards his truck. Gage did not try to break the grip as he was back peddled across the camp yard. He felt a painful jolt as he slammed into the side of his truck.

"Stop it Roy, please stop. Please let me help you," Gage yelled after the momentum halted.

Roy's eyes were dripping with tears and Gage began to lose his composure as well. His voice trembled as he attempted to console his brother by embracing him.

"I.....I love you Roy. I could never ask for a better brother. And, and your kids have the best father in the world."

Roy stood there for a moment, breathing intensely before burying his face into the collar of Gage's jacket. He cried loudly for a long time while his brother held him.

"She's leaving me Gage." Gage continued to hug him tightly.

"I know Roy. We're gonna get you through this."

Even though he didn't understand why, Gage knew how much Roy worshipped Kaylie. She was the love of his life, the only love he had ever known.

Back inside the camp an hour later, Roy told Gage that Kaylie had been having an affair. This made Gage even angrier but he tried to remain composed. Roy finally fell asleep on the couch at 5:00 a.m. Daylight was soon to come so Gage walked into the kitchen to turn off the gas lamp. He saw the gun leaning against the wall inside of the closet as he passed by but didn't think anything of it at first. He picked up the .308 rifle and then walked over to the locked gun cabinet. He released the bolt to make sure it was empty and was very surprised to see a bullet eject from the chamber. Robert Gustafson's number one rule was that loaded guns were not allowed in the camp, and no one had been there since the rabbit hunt earlier that winter. Gage suddenly remembered that it was he who had cleaned all of the rifles on the last day of deer season and placed them into the cabinet. He put his hand over his mouth and looked down at his brother sleeping on the couch.

Roy woke up two hours later and walked outside to a beautiful morning in early spring. Many of the migratory song birds had returned and their calls filled the boreal forest with harmony.

In addition to talking with his brother a few hours before, the thought of his children had also improved his outlook slightly. He was very distraught about his marriage, but for the moment the pain was tolerable. He regretted holding the gun the way he had and began to convince himself, once again, that he would have never pulled the trigger. Never. It was a temporary sense of insanity.

Gage was cutting wood with a splitting mall near the buck pole.

"Gage can you do a favor for me?" Gage turned around, surprised to see Roy awake so early.

"Sure."

"Can you go to my house and pick up the kids? I'm sure they'll want to spend the day out here with me."

"No problem."

Gage knew he needed to ask Roy about the gun so he brought it up nonchalantly before leaving. Roy explained that he saw a bear as he pulled up to the camp, so he loaded the rifle in hopes of getting a shot if it returned. Gage was satisfied and very much relieved by the answer. Roy was a good liar when he needed to be.

Gage thought about the inevitable divorce as he drove towards town. Would Kaylie try to get full custody of the children? Would she get a lawyer and fight Roy for as much money as possible? Roy had asked Gage to pick up a few changes of clothes, and had also given him money to get enough food for a couple of days. He was also asked to convey the news to their parents, which he was certain would break his mother's heart. Gage stopped at the grocery store to pick up supplies for the camp. He assumed that Roy would stay there until the divorce was settled. He walked into his parents' home soon after and explained to them what had happened. Sarah cried and Robert used a number of filthy words to describe his daughter-in-law. Gage hugged his mother and assured her that he would step up and help Roy in whatever way he could. They talked about the tragedy for nearly an hour, but many questions were left unanswered due to legal complexities involved. The most important topic was the welfare of Khora and Otto. The Gustafson's began to conspire about how Roy might be able to obtain full custody. The fact that Kaylie was not a good mother and that she had admitted to infidelity would certainly help.

"Did you find him?" Kaylie asked as Gage walked through the door of his brothers' home.

"He's at camp."

The kids greeted Gage as they always did, with hugs and kisses and questions. When they ran off into the other room Kaylie tried to make eye contact with Gage, but he refused to look directly at her. His anger was starting to get the better of him and he desperately wanted to reveal his opinion about her, but he refrained because of the children.

"How is he doing?" she asked as though she were inquiring about a distant relative.

"He's fine. If you don't mind I'd like to take the children out to the camp, Roy is waiting to see them. He also needs clothes."

Gage was cautious in the way he spoke, he did not want to make Kaylie angry for fear that she may not allow him to take the children.

"That's fine" she said.

Gage knew his way around the house. He packed a bag for Roy and also packed clothes and toys for the kids. He gathered the children up and walked them out the door, failing to say goodbye to Kaylie. She said nothing as they exited the house.

Gage spent the remainder of the weekend with his brother and the kids, watching Roy closely as he attempted to enjoy his children.

Chapter Fifteen

Things had to get worse before they got better. A meeting was arranged between Roy and Kaylie at her attorneys' office four days after she had informed him of her intentions. Kaylie was not wasting any time and Roy was in no mood for a fight. Despite being prompted by his family Roy refused to retain an attorney. He just wanted to get the whole thing over with. He didn't care about the business or the land. The custody of the children would be his only focus. Roy asked Gage to accompany him to the meeting. Gage agreed to go if Roy promised not to agree to any arrangements until he spoke to an attorney afterward.

"Alright" he said.

Roy forced himself to see Dr. Pruett that morning and was very honest about his state of mind and contemplation of suicide. After assuring her he would not have gone through with it, he was prescribed a higher dose of the anti-depressant and promised to return in two weeks. Even though Roy knew the medication was helping him somewhat, he felt weak and guilty about his reliance upon it and was not happy about increasing the dose. But the thought of his cousin Kenneth, who had committed suicide many years prior, convinced him to comply with what Dr. Pruett had asked. Deep in his soul, Roy knew that suicide had become a very realistic option while at camp a few days before.

At 2:00 p.m. on the first Wednesday of May, the brothers walked into Attorney Gavin Miller's office. They were seated in a conference room by a secretary and told that Kaylie and

Mr. Miller would be in shortly. Roy was very despondent. Gage tried to persuade his brother that he must be aggressive when the meeting started, but Roy just stared at the floor silently. Gavin Miller and Kaylie walked into the room a few minutes later. Miller introduced himself and announced that he would be representing Mrs. Gustafson. Gage felt defenseless and he worried that Kaylie would tear her husband apart. She was dressed to kill, wearing a very nice dress and high heel shoes. There was no doubt that Kaylie was a sexually attractive woman; a beautiful, heartless, sexually attractive woman. Miller looked to Roy before speaking.

"Mr. Gustafson, your wife wishes to resolve this in an amicable manner."

Roy did not respond nor did he look at his wife or Gavin Miller. Gage felt the urge to speak.

"My brother has not hired an attorney yet but he will after we hear what you have to say today."

Miller transferred his attention from Roy to Gage.

"Are you here to speak on behalf of your brother?"

"When I need to" said Gage as he stared coldly into the eyes of the attorney.

"Well, this shouldn't take long. Mrs. Gustafson has refused my advice in this matter. She wants to begin a new life and has informed me that she, because of the guilt felt by her actions, she does not want any part of Roy's company. She asks that Roy sell enough land to provide her with $250,000 in cash to pay for college and living expenses over the next four years. Again, she has made this decision on her own against my advice."

Gage was very surprised by what the attorney was saying, he was certain that Roy's company and land was now worth far more than $1.5 million. Gage looked to Roy for a response but it seemed as though he was not paying attention.

"Furthermore," said Miller, "She is willing to remove her name from the title of the house and concede full custody of the children to Roy."

Roy's disposition changed drastically as he sat up straight and looked at the attorney. "What did you say?"

It was obvious that Gavin Miller was not enthused by his client's decision. He opened his hands and elevated them above the table with a sigh.

"She wants $250,000 in exchange for removing her name from any ownership that you share with her, and also agrees to give up all rights to her children."

Kaylie Gustafson sat quietly next to her attorney looking somewhat embarrassed. It was now apparent that she wanted to erase her life completely, including her two children, and start over with no strings attached.

"Alright" said Roy. "I will agree to that right now."

Both Gage and Roy were shocked by the fact that Kaylie wanted no part of her own children. Gavin Miller stood up from his seat and adjourned the meeting after only five minutes of discussion.

"This is the easiest divorce case that I have ever handled. I will draw up the legal documents and forward them to your attorney, whoever that may be, within a few days." As Roy walked out of the conference room he felt Kaylie's hand on his arm, he turned to look at her for the first time in four days. With tears in her eyes she struggled to speak. "Roy, I realize this probably won't mean a lot to you but I'm sorry for what I've done. I could never make you understand that I am not the person who's life I've been living since we married. I've never been able to meet the demands of being a mother and wife. It's just not in me. I'll be out of the house by tomorrow Roy."

He nodded his head and continued to walk out of Gavin Miller's office.

"Goodbye Kaylie."

Chapter Sixteen

The remainder of that first week in May was very hectic for Gage. He began two of his final four courses and the remaining two would begin in June. Because his attention had been concentrated on his brother's problems, Gage had already fallen behind in school. He wasn't worried about it though; the following weekend would be spent locked indoors studying like a rocket scientist. Gage knew that his brother and the children needed him now more than ever so he decided to stop working at the bar on the weekends. He would enjoy the summer semester much more than the winter because his classes seemed to be more interesting and less demanding, and there were fewer of them. Hopefully in September a full time career would be launched, he had already prepared a resume and would soon send them to companies in Michigan and Wisconsin. Gage was eager to build a clientele who would rely on him for investment decisions. He knew that most people, especially those that were in their twenties and thirties, did not save enough to retire by the age of fifty-five or sixty. Pensions were becoming a benefit of the past in the corporate world, and individuals had to rely more on themselves to partially fund 401(k)'s and other such plans. Gage would help clients to accomplish this by providing sound advice and good investment options to choose from. He would use his education and appealing personality to soon become a successful financial advisor. That was the plan, and the plan would be set in motion soon enough. But first he needed to do well during his final semester at NMU.

Roy's attitude had improved slightly after being offered full custody of the children but his broken heart would take a long time to heal. Even though he put on a happy face while spending time with the kids, he was otherwise very depressed. Despite his best efforts, Roy had lost the woman to whom he had dedicated several years of marriage. At least one member of his family either called or visited him every day. But no matter how much he was praised for being a wonderful father and husband, Roy could not be uplifted. He now faced the challenge of raising the children by himself and explaining to them that they would not likely see their mother again. The challenge would be made easier by the fact that Kaylie was not a good mother. The $250,000 payment to her was funded by the sale of one of Roy's favorite pieces of property. It was the first parcel that Roy had obtained, he purchased it one year before marrying Kaylie. The land consisted of a thirty acre lake surrounded by fifty more acres of rolling hardwoods. Roy and Kaylie had planned to someday build a retirement home on a ridge that overlooked the lake. Roy did not want to sell the property but it was a small price to pay for the custodial rights of his children. Because the value of waterfront property had escalated since the purchase, it was sold promptly for $270,000 and the remainder of the profit was used to start a college fund for the kids.

The summer flew by as summers always do. Roy worked four long days during the week and stayed home with Khora and Otto for three. His mother provided further stability by watching the children one day and a day care provider came to his home for the remaining three. Gage helped out when Roy worked late and also on the weekends when Roy had chores to do. Roy gracefully tackled the responsibility of being a single parent. After a hard day's work in the woods, he would provide them with an evening of games, books, and an everlasting supply of love. He was truly an exceptional father, despite his disguised mental illness. The children were also going through a very difficult time, after all,

Kaylie was the only mother they had known and now she was gone forever. Sarah Gustafson filled the motherly void the very best she knew how, and Gage spent much of his free time with Roy and the children.

Gage graduated with honors from Northern Michigan University in August of 1996. Sarah Gustafson was out of her mind with pride for her son, and she threw quite a party for him with all of his friends and relatives attending. Lillian Gauthier, his godmother, was also very proud of Gage.

"I knew you could do it Gage! Now move ahead and capitalize on a great career."

Gage had come a long way. A year and a half earlier, he had not shown any ambition or initiative. He lived for the present day only and spent most of his time doing nothing that anyone would consider to be productive. But the seven month rut was necessary in hindsight because Gage was able to easily build himself again after being forcefully persuaded by his family. And now he was ready for the real world, eager to begin his career in the financial services sector.

Gage had attended an interview in Green Bay one week prior to his graduation party and had been invited to three more during the following week. The upcoming interviews would be held in the Lower Peninsula and even though he was very excited about them, Gage preferred to live in the Upper Peninsula, or in Wisconsin if nothing materialized in the U.P. He had been nervous for the interview in Green Bay and would have rather it not be his first, but in retrospect he thought it went very well. The name of the Green Bay firm was Schumacher and Abel, and Gage was greatly impressed by the two partners and the mission statement of the company. He memorized it word for word:

"Our mission is to provide the investment tools necessary to prompt the basic concept of saving of any individual or private entity. We will concentrate whole heartedly on the best interest of our clients, ensuring that their financial goals are outlined and achieved by merely paying themselves first. We refuse to chase the commission of high risk, poorly performing options but instead will rely upon the purchase of reliable and consistent offerings of the world's greatest companies. Furthermore, no client will be neglected. We pledge to pay special attention to those who have financial problems, of which they have not been able to overcome on their own. A strategy will be devised to consolidate debt and to create the necessary financial responsibility, thus placing them on a path that will lead to a fruitful retirement."

Gage was particularly impressed by the pledge to help those who are in financial distress; this statement conveyed that Schumacher and Abel were in the business to help those who have not yet been able to help themselves.

The celebration turned into a Yooper dance shortly after supper, provoked by the fast feet of Gage's father. Robert was also very proud of his son. His pride was displayed by first dancing by himself and then with anyone who was willing. Soon the patio was filled with a cheerful crowd, of which some were poor dancers and others who were awful. Gage laughed as he enjoyed the entertainment while seated beside his good friend Dave. Gage was worried about Dave, he had not yet found a good job after being let go from the sawmill two years earlier. He was currently employed part-time by a small roofing company that paid a less than average wage and provided no health or retirement benefits. And since Gage had found himself and was now ecstatic about his future, he felt compelled to help his friend do the same.

"Dave, I want to talk to you about something." David had already consumed a number of beers but was still able to carry on a sensible conversation.

"What is it pal?"

Gage put down his beer and leaned over towards his friend.

"I know that you want to stay in the U.P. as much or even more than I do. The timing is not the greatest right now because my brother just went through a divorce, and I wish I was able to get a job nearby in order for me to help with the kids. But I have to follow my dream. The truth is that there are not many good jobs up here so most of us are forced to either take a shitty job at home, or move elsewhere. You've been waiting two years for a call from the iron ore mine Dave, but there's no guarantee that you'll get that call. And even if you do, many people say that the mines won't even be here twenty years down the line."

"Are you giving me a pep talk Gage?"

"Yah, I guess I am but it's only because I care a lot about you Dave."

"Gage, are you gay?" asked David.

"No I'm not gay, I'm trying to help you Dave."

"Because if you are gay I'm alright with that. All of us guys have noticed that you haven't had a girlfriend in a long time, and we've also noticed that you enjoy hugging your friends more than a man normally would."

"I'm not gay, dammit! You've been drinking a lot and fucking around and your life is starting to pass you by David" said Gage in a serious tone.

David's expression changed from one of sympathy to hurtfulness.

"That's not very nice Gage."

"I'm sorry Dave, but I think you need to get the hell out of here. You've got a lot of skills that could land you a good job where such jobs can be found. I have a proposal for you. I'm hopeful that I'll be offered a job in Wisconsin or the Lower Peninsula, and I want you to come with me. We could share an apartment and we'll both have good jobs that we can be proud of. It'll be easy to save money and we'll be able to buy some land up here in a few years."

"What do you say Davey boy?"

It was immediately apparent that Gage's proposal had kicked David's mind into high gear. He moved his fingers through the goat tee that had been spared after the conclusion of the prior deer season, and stared absently straight ahead. Gage was taken back by the obvious moment of deep thought; he had not witnessed such a revelation in Dave before.

"You don't have to answer me now Dave, I don't even know where I'm going yet."

"I'll do it!" Dave suddenly shouted. "You're right about moving away from here. There's more to life than fishing and hunting, it's time for me to get started on a career also. I'm in Gage, I'm in!"

Dave and Gage made a toast with two cans of Miller High Life and shook hands.

"You know Gage, I just want to tell you that you're the best friend a man could ever ask for. I love you man."

Dave embraced Gage with a bear hug.

"I love you too Dave" Gage smirked. "And now I know we can get an apartment with just one bedroom!"

Dave didn't laugh.

Roy was seated nearby with a smile, entertained by the conversation between Gage and his good friend. The higher dosage of medication his doctor had prescribed was working well, and although heartbroken, Roy was optimistic about his family's future. Khora and Otto proved to be resilient and were making great strides in recent weeks.

On the following morning, Gage was in his apartment preparing more cover letters and resume's to be mailed. He would continue to mail them until he was offered a job, no chances would be taken. Arrangements had already been made to begin a monthly payment for his college loans. He needed to obtain a job within two months so that he could fulfill the payment schedule. Gage was like his mother in that he worried a lot. He worried about Roy and the children, and now he began to suddenly worry about not finding a job. After all, if a person did not do well during an interview they simply would not get the job, no matter how well equipped they were. An unfair fact of life.

Gage had somehow misplaced his official college transcripts so he decided to make one last trip to NMU to get more. He arrived at the parking lot of the records office to a bustling crowd of students who had just begun the fall semester. The sight pleased him and he realized that he would miss the life of a college student. He emerged from his truck and immediately noticed a familiar face. It was Kaylie Gustafson, and she was sitting on the hood of a car with a man in her arms. A feeling of rage overtook Gage that was similar to what he felt the night he caught Sherri Anderson with another man. Kaylie had already granted full legal custody to Roy with no rights of survivorship, so Gage decided to take the opportunity to tell her just what he thought. He walked up behind them and then introduced himself to her boyfriend. Kaylie was greatly surprised.

"Hi there" Gage said as he held out his hand to the stranger.

"My name is Gage Gustafson and Kaylie here is my ex-sister in law."

The man shook Gage's hand and said hello reluctantly. Gage then put his arm around him as though he were his best friend.

"I just thought I'd let you know that you're dating a tramp who cheated on my brother, probably with you but maybe not, and then abandoned him and their two wonderful children. Even worse, she willingly gave up full custody of her children in exchange for a lump sum payment of $250,000."

Gage spoke as though he was giving everyday financial advice to a future client.

"So if you want a woman with some money but absolutely no moral values whatsoever, here she is. I just thought you would want to know pal."

The man's eyes became as big as saucers as he looked from Gage to Kaylie. It was obvious that he didn't know the full story. Gage also looked to Kaylie and then padded the stranger on the back as he pivoted to walk away.

"Hell is only half full Kaylie, I hope I don't have to join you there."

When Gage returned to his apartment the answering machine on the phone was blinking. He pressed the button to retrieve his messages while still in a state of astonishment from what he had said to Kaylie's boyfriend. He didn't regret it because he had controlled the urge to do so on many occasions for quite some time. The first message was from his mother, asking if he needed a new suit for his upcoming interviews. The second was from a company in Milwaukee, calling to set up an interview. The third message caused Gage to shake with excitement; it was Timothy Abel from the firm of Abel and Shumacher in Green Bay. Gage quickly picked up the receiver and dialed the number.

"Hello, this is Gage Gustafson returning Mr. Abel's phone call."

A few minutes later, Gage was offered and immediately accepted a position with the firm. His beginning salary was $33,200 and he was told that the figure would increase substantially if he performed well. He would report to work just two weeks later, on September 15th of 1996.

Gage didn't bother to get into his truck. He put on his shoes and ran north through the streets of downtown Ishpeming towards his parent's home. He screamed with joy many times as he sprinted for a half mile, his mind full of all the wonderful things to come. Gage burst through the door to announce the news to his parents and his mother ran down the front hall stairs to embrace him. Gage couldn't help it; he started to cry as she held him. Gage Gustafson was the happiest man on earth. Robert stood at the top of the stairs with a piece of Trenary toast in his hand and a wide grin across his face.

"That's my boy" he said.

Gage called everyone he knew that night and then went over to his brother's house. Roy gave him an enthusiastic hand shake and then invited him to sit on the porch to celebrate with a beer and a pinch of Copenhagen snuff.

"I knew you could do it Gage. We're very fortunate that you will be only three hours from home."

The kids were the only recipients of the news that were not happy about it. Gage did his best to explain that he needed to go, but that he would definitely be home on most weekends. They didn't understand and demanded that he move home as quickly as possible.

"That's my plan down the road" he promised.

Gage and David scoured the classified ads of the Green Bay newspaper on the following day and decided to soon drive down to look at apartments. Dave was almost as excited as Gage and was greatly enthused by the number and variety of jobs available in the Green Bay area. He made some phone calls and set up interviews for two days later. Gage helped him to build a resume' that would be appealing to the manufacturing sector. David was overtaken by a new and pleasant feeling of responsibility as he researched career possibilities on the internet.

The trip to Wisconsin passed by quickly as they discussed everything from jobs to hunting to women. One woman in particular, Josie Strong, was talked about for quite some time. After being encouraged by David, Gage decided that he would call Josie Strong again after things settled down. He had not forgotten about their brief meeting on New Year's Eve and hoped that she hadn't either. She seemed like the perfect girl, but Gage could not understand why she had not returned the phone call several months earlier.

The day in Green Bay went very well, they found a small two bedroom apartment and David landed a job as an intern machinist. They would make their final move on that following Friday so they would have the weekend to settle in before their jobs started. So they returned to Ishpeming with a little over a week to enjoy themselves. Gage decided that he would spend as much time as possible with his niece and nephew during that week.

Gage took advantage of the following eight days. He spent a lot of time with the kids knowing they were still troubled by the fact that Kaylie had abandoned them. They asked him many questions about her, most of which he could not answer with total honesty, attempting to protect them from the ugliness of real life. Roy's outlook was improving and he started to once again spend time with those he cared for other than the children. He invited Gage to spend a day with him at work and Gage gladly accepted. He was very interested in how his brother was able to purchase so much land and figured he would learn much. And he did. Roy picked him up at 7:00 a.m. and they visited two logging jobs where his crews were working. Gage met all fifteen of Roy's employees and immediately sensed a great deal of mutual respect between them and the man they worked for. Roy explained the basics of logging which Gage was already somewhat familiar with. He then showed him the difference in the value of each type of merchantable tree, based upon whether utilized for pulp, bolts, or sawlogs. Gage found the marketing portion of the logging industry to be very interesting. In addition to the real estate portion of the business, this was Roy's primary responsibility. He negotiated prices for his wood with various mills that were located in the U.P. and northern Wisconsin. He also had a strong customer base from other areas of the United States and even from outside of the country. These buyers were interested in the highest quality logs only, such as bird's eye maple, curly maple, and number one veneer. After they were sold, such logs would be transported all over the world to be used for the construction of musical instruments, very expensive furniture, and other items. Gage was impressed by his brother's knowledge and marketing tactics while attending a meeting with a log buyer from Japan later that morning. He didn't realize that people from Japan actually visited the Upper Peninsula. It also struck him that his position with Abel and Schumacher would be similar in many respects to what Roy did. Gage was a stock broker, and his brother was a producer and salesman of logs and pulpwood. Roy conveyed to Gage that the retirement funds of he and his employees would be transferred to Gage's employer, they would be his first clients and Gage was very excited and thankful.

The afternoon was spent looking at several pieces of property for sale in Marquette County. Gage listened carefully as Roy compared the asking price to the value he believed the land to be worth. Roy's evaluation of each parcel was based on the location, surrounding ownership type, and most importantly, the value of standing timber. They walked five parcels and Roy determined that none of them were even remotely close to being a good value. Each of the parcels had been cut much too hard, mismanaged, and it would take decades to grow the timber back to a sustainable value.

"It's becoming very difficult to find a fair price on land anymore" Roy said.

"We've spent about five man hours looking at land for nothing, so in essence I have lost money for the day. And it may take me another forty hours of driving and walking to find a piece worth buying, but that piece will turn one hell of a profit over the long haul."

Gage understood entirely because buying a solid growth stock was a similar endeavor.

A more serious topic emerged in the truck during the drive back to Ishpeming.

"Gage, I've asked my attorney to draft a new will because of the divorce."

"That's a good idea Roy" responded Gage.

"If I were to die for some reason, you would inherit my business and all of the real estate owned by the Gustafson Land and Log Company."

Gage didn't know what to say so he remained quiet, expecting that Roy wasn't finished.

"Also and most importantly, you would be granted full custody of the children in the event of my death. Mom and Dad are getting too old to handle something like that, I wouldn't want to burden them. I wanted to see how you feel about this before the will is finalized and recorded. You have the makings of a great father Gage, the kids adore you."

Gage was the godfather of both Khora and Otto, but he had never thought about being their primary caregiver. He felt himself becoming emotional but was able to hold back. Roy and he had just cried together a few months before, once in a lifetime was enough.

"I appreciate that Roy. I would be honored to take care of the kids if you passed away. But fortunately, we'll never have to worry about that."

"Let's hope not, but I don't want there to be any chance of Kaylie getting custody if I die" said Roy.

Gage felt the need to lighten the conversation.

"But if you do die, can I sell the land and company and go live with some hookers in Detroit?"

"Not funny asshole" said Roy with a smile.

Chapter Seventeen

That evening Gage decided to make his last trip to the grocery store before departing for Green Bay a few days later. As he roamed the store aimlessly, confused as to what he should prepare for upcoming meals, he heard a familiar voice.

"Hi Gage."

Josie Strong smiled at him reluctantly from the end of the aisle.

"Josie. Well….Hi, how are you."

She was even more beautiful than he remembered.

"I'm great" she responded confidently.

"I just finished up with school and now I'm home for a few weeks."

Gage was completely caught off guard by her presence. He also became instantly prideful and stubborn while remembering that she had not returned his phone call months before. Gage also sensed a negative tone from Josie when she spoke to him and his cautious demeanor towards women kicked in, and he quickly decided to flee. "Well….I'll see you around then Josie."

Josie paused for a moment, allowing him time to reconsider but Gage was silent. "Goodbye Gage."

Gage decided that he didn't need any groceries and quickly walked toward the exit of the store. He was confused as to why Josie was being abrasive towards him and immediately concluded that she was not interested. After all, she hadn't returned his phone call and he was not about to make another attempt. She hadn't even apologized and he believed she must have been dating someone in Minnesota. He walked out of the store hastily, feeling hurt and embarrassed.

"Fuckin' women" Gage mumbled under his breath as he approached his truck.

"Gage!" Josie yelled from behind him.

Gage turned to see her quickly approaching him. He was caught by surprise yet again. "What?" he responded in a loud and unfriendly tone.

"So that's it then?" she said. "New Years' Eve was just a big joke then right Gage?" "What are you talking about Josie? I called you soon after and you didn't call me back."

"You never called me Gage."

"Yes I did, I left a message with your brother."

"Well....Well he never gave me the message."

Josie's attitude quickly turned from anger to curiosity.

"So you tried to call me then?"

"I sure did."

They both smiled broadly at the exact same time as each realized the other was still very much interested. Josie didn't waste any time, she closed the gap between them and stared at him with her beautiful hazel eyes.

"I am going to kill my brother! I'm really happy you called Gage, I've been thinking about you constantly and had a difficult time finishing up with college."

"Me too Josie" he said nervously as he reached for her.

So there in the parking lot of Jim's IGA the two embraced for minutes and then their lips met for only the second time ever. Gage embraced her and they began to involve themselves in a very sexual endeavor. The darkness of night had arrived. They were briefly interrupted by employees leaving the store after closing, but continued aggressively shortly thereafter. Gage lifted Josie easily, his testosterone pumping wildly, and slid her into the back seat of his truck. While doing so he frantically brushed away shotgun shells, hunting clothes and a fishing creel as Josie chuckled at him nervously.

"I'm sorry it's so messy in here."

"I don't care Gage, I don't care at all."

They undressed each other slowly without allowing their lips to part, and then made passionate love for quite some time. It was the right decision, each knowing full well that this was the very beginning of a wonderful relationship.

After some time had passed and the two became very close, Gage began to occasionally tease Josie about having sex with him before their first official date. Josie was not usually tolerant of the teasing and argued that she believed they were in fact dating from the very first moment they saw one another, in the bar on New Years' Eve.

Gage and Josie spent much time together over the next few days. The Gustafson family adored her and Gage's mother was very enthused about the new development in his life. The good news continued for Gage when he found out that Josie had accepted a teaching position in Appleton, Wisconsin, just twenty miles from his apartment in Green Bay.

As promised, Gage took Josie on several proper dates including hiking trips to Pictured Rocks and the Keweenaw Peninsula, of which they both enjoyed very much. Discussions were almost constant and they quickly became knowledgeable of the others aspirations and fears. Gage was very impressed at how quickly the children took to Josie, she had a very loving personality that all children desire. Although agreeing that they shouldn't move too hastily into a serious relationship, neither Gage nor Josie had any reservations to speak of; they were undoubtedly falling in love.

Josie and Gage's family met him and David at the apartment to bid them farewell on the day of their departure. Josie would be following Gage to Wisconsin just one month later and had already arranged an apartment with a roommate in Appleton. Gage bought presents for Khora and Otto and once again promised that he would be home often to see them. He shook the hands of a proud brother and father, embraced Josie, and then hugged his mom for a long time. Gage could see her crying in the rear view mirror of his truck as he pulled away with a U-Haul trailer following behind. Sarah Gustafson cried partially because she was so very proud of her son, and partially because her baby was entirely on his own. Roy held her closely.

"You sure have a wonderful family Gage" David said. "I wish I did."

"You will soon enough Dave, you will make it happen."

Roy Gustafson was compelled to spend some time alone the weekend after his brother departed, at the family deer camp. Even though his favorite time of year was approaching, the depression had intensified suddenly with a vengeance. The increased dose of the anti-depressant, prescribed to Roy just before the divorce, had definitely benefitted his outlook as he struggled to move his family forward. But now hopelessness had returned again without warning and he had no urge to be in the company of those that he so dearly loved.

Anguish had begun to consume him once again, and he thought it may have been prompted by his brother's departure. He and the kids would miss Gage very much. Roy had been in this state of mind on many occasions throughout his adult life, and being alone at this favorite place in the world would likely help him. He needed to pray and think, while locating himself far from any sound of civilization.

An agonizing and familiar mental battle was waged for hours after arriving at the camp. He attempted to concentrate on all of the wonderful things God had provided; two wonderful children, great parents and a supportive brother, a thriving business and a beautiful home. As he had many times in the past, Roy wondered how a sense of depression could undermine the many positive aspects of his life, how had hopelessness so easily returned? The opener of ruffed grouse season was only a few days away and yet he felt no excitement for the anticipation of his favorite outdoor pastime.

Other than a light roar from the burning fire, absolute quietness overcame the atmosphere on that cool day in September. He welcomed the solitude, slowly and after several hours it began to improve his mindset after again convincing himself just how good life really was. But Roy knew it wouldn't last, he knew from painful experience that symptoms would return again without warning.

There at camp Roy thought about a local man named Richie, a well-known resident who managed a popular gas station in town. Richie knew everyone and everyone knew Richie, mostly because of his loving and contagious personality. Roy admired him. Most would not consider to be intelligent, nor was he visibly attractive, and he earned far less than an average wage at the gas station. He lived alone in a very small house just a block from the gas station and could not afford a vehicle. Anyone who didn't know Richie might think his sense of happiness was minimal; no notable accomplishments to speak of, no fame or glory had ever found him, and he did not have enough money to afford luxuries. But Richie's personality was invaluable, his outlook was unmatched. His sense of humor, his endlessly positive attitude and sincere interest in the lives of all who visited the gas station was an anomaly.

Rather than thinking of himself and how he could benefit his own life, Richie was a giver, an overcomer. Despite the loss of his wife to cancer when she was in her early forties, he refused to relent to grief and instead strived to make the lives of others better. Richie was a leader at a church in Ishpeming and many believed that his permanent smile and attitude were delivered by God himself. Church was not where his best work was done however, but rather at the old gas station in town where hundreds of patrons stopped by weekly. Richie made it his business to know every resident patron by name; he knew of their children's hobbies and aspirations and served as a mentor to nearly everyone at one time or another. And because he constantly demanded from himself a loving and caring personality towards others, Richie was by far the happiest man in town, deeply loved by all.

"If only I could be more like Richie." Roy said quietly to himself. "I would give up this business and land if I could have his outlook on life."

Chapter Eighteen

September 15th was the first day of ruffed grouse season in Michigan, but Gage didn't think about hunting even once during his first day at work. He had become a responsible young man with wonderful prospects, and was dressed to match those prospects with a sharp looking suit and tie. Tim Abel and Eric Schumacher, the owners of the firm, welcomed him with a very courteous reception. After he was escorted to his office and explained more about the aspects of his job over a three hour period, Gage was introduced to the other nine employees of the firm. An extended luncheon was held for him and he had the opportunity to meet with each advisor to discuss their responsibilities within the company. Gage was nervous at first but soon felt very comfortable with his counterparts. Each one of them conveyed that Abel and Schumacher were the finest bosses they had ever worked for. That meant a great deal to Gage. He could suddenly see himself working there for thirty years and then retiring back in his beloved Upper Peninsula. His office was spacious and extravagant and on his desk was a piece of paper with the names and phone numbers of potential new clients that had recently contacted the firm. The receptionist explained to him that numerous potential customers were from a diverse demographic of varying needs. Some were young adults who wanted to enroll in a 401(k) savings plan, and others were older individuals that sought financial guidance or were about to retire and desired to purchase annuities through the company.

Gage stayed very late that night and spoke to all twenty-eight people that had recently inquired, of which twenty-four committed to upcoming meetings to potentially set up accounts with him. Although he felt a bit overwhelmed, his confidence increased by the hour and his natural ability to solidify client relationships would soon be obvious to Abel and Schumacher. He also began to work on transferring the retirement accounts of his brother and the employees of his growing business, now totaling twenty people.

Gage and David met back at the apartment at 9:00 p.m. that night and both were equally excited and exhausted. Dave's first day at work sparked an attitude that Gage had not witnessed in quite some time, he was very enthused about his future with the small fabricating company that now employed him, and spoke positively about his supervisors and co-workers. They celebrated with non-stop conversation over a glass of fine Wisconsin beer for quite some time, and then Gage called Josie to fill her in before turning in for the night.

The following morning at 8:00 a.m. Gage sat down with Abel, Schumacher and the receptionist to handle additional employment paperwork. He updated them on his work the afternoon before and they were greatly impressed with the number of potential clients that had agreed to meet with him, and were especially thrilled about signing up all employees of the Gustafson Land and Log Company.

"You're going to be a rock star Gage. If you keep up this pace you'll get a dandy bonus long before your first anniversary with us, and that's a promise my friend."

Eric Schumacher smiled as he exited the room.

After lunch at his desk that early afternoon, Gage took a moment to enjoy the view of a bustling city from his office window and then decided to step outside. Even though his days had been packed with excitement, he thought about Josie Strong often. He was surprised at how much he missed her and hoped that he would someday be lucky enough to marry her. She would arrive in Wisconsin a few weeks later and he could barely wait to see her. He was also missing his niece and nephew and planned to call them that night to check in. He was hopelessly attached.

After watching Sherri Anderson walk by and reflecting on his life for a while, he entered the office again for a long afternoon of exciting work. The phone rang as he arrived at his desk; it was another logging company owner from the Upper Peninsula. Eric Fredy explained to Gage that he desired to start a retirement program for each of his fourteen employees, he had been given Gage's phone number by his brother Roy. As Gage began explaining the process and options to Fredy after thanking him for the call, the door to his office was opened and the receptionist quickly walked in with a serious expression on her face. She put her hand up to get his attention but Gage held out his index finger with a smile to indicate that he was on an important call.

"Gage...Gage I'm sorry to interrupt but I have an urgent call for you."

"Can I call you back shortly Mr. Fredy?" said Gage over the phone as a concerned expression overcame him.

He quickly placed the phone on the receiver and then asked "What is it Trisha?"

"I'm putting the call through to you now."

Trisha walked briskly from his office to connect the call. Gage picked up the phone on the first half-ring.

"Hello, this is Gage Gustafson." Gage immediately became very concerned when he heard the familiar exhale of his father, but this time his breathing was broken by short bursts of hyperventilation.

"Gage...Gage my boy" said Robert Gustafson as he struggled to speak.

"Dad? Dad what is it, are you ok? Is mom ok?"

"Gage it's your brother...It's your brother Roy.....He's gone Gage."

Gage began to shake uncontrollably while struggling to comprehend what he had just been told.

"What do you mean Dad? What are you saying?... Is Roy dead?"

Gage heard a deep broken sigh before his father responded.

"He has taken his own life Gage...I'm....I'm so sorry."

Gage hung up the phone with his right hand as his trembling left hand covered his mouth. His disbelief was covered in tears as he rose from his desk, unsure of what to do or where to go. He paced back and forth while weeping quietly, and the heightening shock and disbelief almost caused him to pick up the phone to return the call to Fredy. He struggled fiercely to accept the news for the next several minutes as he twitched and trembled, often running his fingers quickly through his hair, almost violently.

Gage later found out that his cousin John had found Roy at the deer camp that morning, lying dead near the front porch with a fatal gun-shot wound to his chest and his own .308 caliber rifle in the deep grass beside him. John Gustafson was so distraught that he was admitted for two days to Bell Hospital due to shock, and was treated with medication to cope with the unbearable sight he had stumbled upon.

The receptionist, Trisha Baldwin, entered Gage's office again and immediately embraced him as he sputtered the terrible news. Gage asked her not to tell anyone in the office until he was gone; his only immediate need was to get home to his family. Trisha called Dave at work after Gage provided her with the number, and Dave drove him back to Ishpeming. Despite Dave's repeated efforts to console him during the three hour drive, Gage wept quietly and was not able to speak, other than two words that he muttered from time to time.

"The kids.....The kids."

Chapter Nineteen

The following days, weeks and months were brutal for the Gustafson family and time did not begin to heal them. Josie remained at Gage's side every moment until she was forced to leave for the teaching position in Wisconsin, and he cried in her embrace several times each day. But he knew that strength would need to be portrayed in front of Roy's children and even Sarah and Robert Gustafson. Sarah was hopelessly heartbroken and stayed in bed for nearly a week, although she gathered enough strength to spend some time with her confused grandchildren each day. She read to them, caressed them, and promised them that everything would be ok. Otto and Khora were too young to comprehend suicide so they were told their father died in a logging accident. Sarah appeared to age ten years overnight and she lost weight which made her already light frame appear to be very fragile.

Robert Gustafson attempted to be the leader of his family as he always had been in the past, but even he could not tolerate the pain and became very quiet and despondent. He began to drink heavily each day in an effort to dull the agony, and spent most of his time sorting through pictures of his lost son. Like Sarah, he also tried to console and cheer up his grandchildren but could only do so for short periods of time. He was weak, and his willingness to live on had faded.

The Gustafson family was in shambles.

Dozens of friends and relatives visited the beloved family each week and John repeatedly attempted to convince his cousin and uncle to visit their camp for a few days to get away, but to no avail. No one visited the camp during the autumn season of 1996 nor was the property accompanied by hunters during deer season in November for the first time ever. Robert and Gage could not visit the camp after great memories there had turned to darkness and death. Every day was filled with sadness and disbelief and to all it seemed the good life was over forever.

Gage Gustafson, with the aid of his soul mate Josie, became a rock for the grieving family. He had no other choice and would only allow himself to fall apart in the company of Josie while she visited on the weekends. And he did so often.

Gage also confided in Dave by phone which also helped him to cope with the immeasurable loss. Dave had made a significant turn in his life and his career was moving ahead rapidly; he had his eye on becoming a supervisor at the machine shop where he was employed.

Even though he was upset with God for allowing such a tragedy to occur, Gage prayed several times each day and spoke to his dead brother in an attempt to retain his sanity. An immense amount of fortitude was somehow gathered and Gage became an effective counselor for the children and his parents. He knew to put the children far before himself and was a constant motivation for happiness in their lives. The months passed by slowly but slight improvements were materializing. Gage slept in his brother's bed each night with the children, they sang together and talked about Roy each night before falling asleep in the arms of one another. No matter how he felt on any given day Gage insisted that his love would provide a gleam of hope for each member of his family. It is what his brother would have asked of him.

Gage knew that he could not return to Wisconsin, there was no decision to be made. He had mustered the will to call his employer two weeks after Roy's death and explained to Tim Abel that he could not return any time in the foreseeable future.

The firm had sent flowers to the funeral and all employees sent individual cards, as though they had known Gage for a very long time.

"Your job will be waiting for you Gage, no matter how much time you need" said Abel as they ended the call.

Time passed and Gage was required to involve himself in Roy's logging business, he handled payroll and talked with each of the crew supervisors daily to ensure that all was well. Roy had assembled a tremendous work force and the logging portion of the company needed little tending from Gage.

Finally after some months, Robert and Sarah Gustafson exhibited minor improvements in their demeanor and began to smile with the children occasionally. Robert broke his temporary addiction to alcohol after Gage confronted him about it.

"The kids need you dad. Mom needs you. I know it's hard but you must continue to live on for them, it's what Roy would have wanted from you."

It became painfully apparent to Gage that his mother and father would not ever be the same after the loss of their eldest son.

Chapter Twenty

On May 16th of 1997, eight months after his brother died, Gage received a phone call from an old friend.

"Hi Gage, how the hell are you?"

It was Jake Steede, a long-time pal who had signed up for the military shortly after graduating from high school and had been a soldier ever since. He and Gage were close friends but had gone their separate ways after high school and only saw each other occasionally, but managed to speak over the phone a few times each year.

"Gage, I just found out about your brother. I'm very sorry."

Jake was calling from a military base in Germany.

"Thanks Jake, it's nice to hear from you. I'm sorry I didn't let you know myself."

"How is your family holding up?" Jake asked.

"Oh we're doing a little better every day and the kids are starting to come around."

The two old friends spoke about the children and Jake's military career for a while, and Jake promised to call Gage the next time he was home.

"Yah, I was home in September of last year but I didn't get to see anyone except my family, you know how that goes. I did take a ride to your camp on the day that I left for Germany, hoping that I might find you there. There were two vehicles parked there but no one was in the camp so I turned around and left."

"Was one of those vehicles mine?" Gage asked.

"No, I recognized your brother's old truck but there was a blue Ford Explorer there that I did not recognize. It had Florida plates."

Gage immediately began to feel sick.

"Florida plates?" he asked.

"Yes, a Ford Explorer."

"Do you remember what day that was Jake?"

"Sure I remember, it was a sad day for me, the day I had to leave for Germany. It was Tuesday, September 16th."

Gage dropped the phone as he assembled what Jake had just told him. Tuesday, September 16th of 1996 would never be forgotten. It was the day that his brother had died. A horrified expression overcame Gage as he recalled the disturbing story that Roy told him about the two men from Florida that he purchased land from. He ended the phone call with Jake Steede without telling him that he had visited the camp on the very day of his brother's death. It was a Ford Explorer with Florida plates that was parked on the road by Roy's property when he returned to his truck after cruising timber some time before. Gage remembered Roy telling him so.

Gage sat down in his brother's recliner with the children on his lap. He collected his thoughts while they watched a cartoon on television. It became suddenly obvious that his brother had not likely committed suicide but was rather a victim of a murder. Tears streamed down his eyes as the shocking truth of that fateful day in September struck him. Gage walked to Roy's office and opened a file cabinet that held all of the information regarding land purchases. He found a folder that had "Fence Road Piece" scribbled on it in permanent marker, and opened it to investigate the information inside. The warranty deed for the land was read and the Florida address of the Richards' brothers was written down. Gage's body was shaking as he picked up the phone to call Trooper Tornberg, a family friend, of the Michigan State Police in the nearby town of Negaunee. He dialed the number and then placed the phone gently back on the receiver before there was an answer. Gage needed time to think.

During their last conversation several months before, Trooper Tornberg had informed Gage that Roy's death was confirmed as a suicide. The gun was returned to Robert Gustafson and he burned it shortly after. Gage had told the Trooper that Roy had no enemies that he could think of, and he also conveyed that Roy had been deeply depressed because of the divorce with Kaylie. Gage had unknowingly given the Trooper even more reason to suspect a suicide by telling him about the night he found Roy at the deer camp and about the rifle that was left in plain view. Gage had found Roy's anti-depressant medication after his death which further supported suicide as the cause of death. Gage laid his head down on the desk in his brother's office and wept.

"They killed you Roy" he said quietly to himself.

"They killed you."

That night, Gage tucked the kids into bed a bit later but was unable to fall asleep himself. The anger in his heart was growing rapidly as he contemplated what needed to be done. He knew it would be very unlikely for the police to prove the Richard's had killed his brother. There was no evidence because the gun was destroyed but there was a $30,000 motive. Roy had refused to pay them the extra money demanded; they must have returned to Ishpeming to intimidate him and then took his life for the sake of revenge. They must have followed Roy to the camp on that day in September. Gage decided to investigate further before going to the authorities or his family. The next morning he logged onto the internet at the library and searched for the phone number of Brett and Frank Richards. After only ten minutes of searching through various web sites, Gage found out that they had recently moved from Florida to the Lower Peninsula of Michigan. He searched by the names of each brother individually to confirm that they lived at the same address in the town of Gaylord.

Gage knew that Trooper Tornberg would aggressively follow up on this new information if he was called. But he also knew that an unproven motive and the word of Jake Steede would definitely not add up to a circumstantial conviction. Gage could trust Josie and desperately wanted to tell her about his suspicions but something told him to keep it all to himself.

It began to eat him alive.

Over the next few days Gage continued to assess hypothetical scenarios of what had been done to his beloved brother, and also what he would potentially do next. His anger grew more intense by the day and it began to totally consume him, partially because he could not share it with anyone. He was able to hide his distress from most, but Josie knew immediately that something was wrong when she returned from her job in Wisconsin for a short vacation. Gage was very quiet and somewhat distracted by his thoughts while he and Josie watched the kids playing one evening. She and Gage had brought the children to the park on one of the first pleasant evenings during the latter part of May.

"Gage, what's wrong? I can tell that something is bothering you."

"Oh, nothing, I've just not been sleeping well lately" Gage responded in an attempt to convince her otherwise.

"You have been very quiet and despondent on the phone lately. Is there something that you want to talk about?" Josie asked.

Gage couldn't hold it in any longer. He needed Josie to hold him; he needed to grieve for his brother once again. Gage tucked his head into her neck and auburn hair and she wrapped her arms tightly around him. The tears were shed quietly and Josie assumed the pain caused by the loss of his brother was the sole reason. But this time it was different. This time the tears were shed in an attempt to deflect the anger and hate that attacked and overwhelmed his soul.

"Josie I need to spend some time alone. I shouldn't leave the kids but I need to figure some things out. I'm going crazy inside."

Josie fully supported Gage's decision. She told him that she and his mother would have no problem looking after the kids for a few days.

"Where are you going to go Gage?" she asked.

"I'm thinking about heading up to the McCormick Tract to camp out for a night or two, I need to clear my head."

Gage had already devised a plan, but it did not involve sleeping in a tent at the McCormick Tract - although this would serve as a convincing alibi.

A few days prior, Gage again visited the Carnegie Public Library on Main Street to carry out more research on the whereabouts and status of the Richards' brothers. Such investigating was never done from his home computer to ensure there would be absolutely no link between he and they. On that day Gage discovered that Frank Richards had died of a drug overdose some weeks before. This fact was very important in that it made development of a plan much less complicated than it otherwise would have been.

Chapter Twenty-One

On a Wednesday in late May, Gage dropped off the children at his parents' house at noon. He had explained beforehand that he needed a day or two on his own, and they agreed that it would be good for him. Sarah and Robert would watch the children during the day and Josie would relieve them during the evenings while home on vacation. Gage bid farewell to the children, who had made impressive strides since the death of their father, and made his way north to the McCormick Tract.

The McCormick Tract, a federally protected wilderness area comprised of 17,000 acres of rugged habitat, was a great choice for those seeking beauty and solitude. The impressive history of the McCormick Tract began in 1884, and that history along with hidden brook trout streams brought Gage and Roy there together on many occasions.

Gage travelled towards Big Bay and then headed west eventually arriving at the Triple A road, a desolate but attractive area, and passed by only one logging truck on his way. He arrived in a remote area near the headwaters of the Yellow Dog River and unloaded the camping supplies and back pack from the bed of his truck, and then removed his fishing pole and creel from the cab. It was a bit early to fish for brook trout on the Yellow Dog River because of the immense amount of spring runoff in Northern Marquette County, but Gage intended to try his luck anyway. Another small back pack was left behind the seat in the truck, the contents of which would be used that night for a more important purpose. He used his compass and walked briskly through an old growth forest for a distance of nearly a mile, and then stopped at a suitable site adjacent to the river. The small tent was erected and supplies were unloaded from the back pack and arranged.

Gage sat down and thought about his brother. He knew that if Roy were seated next to him at that very moment, he would plead with Gage to erase the plan that he had in mind. He would make him promise not to take the law into his own hands, but instead call Trooper Tornberg to inform him of what he knew. But Gage was blinded by hate, so blinded that he would risk everything to bring justice for the murder of his brother. He did not imagine the children, his parents, or Josie without him because his mind had not functioned rationally since the truth was discovered. He walked to the river where he and his brother had fished together long before, and began to cast a minnow in a deep hole. Because he was preoccupied with thoughts of revenge he lost interest in fishing after a short time. His mind was so immersed in thought that he was able to sit and do nothing else, and yet not feel any sense of laziness. Every detail of the plan was neatly arranged in his mind, again and again, and it was now time for implementation.

The growing season had begun even in the north country of the Upper Peninsula. Leaves were beginning to emerge from the buds of the sugar maple and red oak that towered over his camp site. Most of the snow had melted and found its' way to the Yellow Dog River, which was at flood stages typical of any given spring. Gage started a small fire within a ring of rocks near the tent, and then put it out just before the sun disappeared behind the Huron Mountains to the west. It would be dark by the time he reached his truck so he began to make his way there. It was just after 8:00 p.m. when he arrived at the vehicle which was parked on a grown over logging spur adjacent to the main gravel road. He paused for a moment to listen for the unlikely sound of other vehicles, and then started his truck and drove off. He was in no hurry because there was plenty of time to do what needed to be done. The drive to Gaylord would be about 5 hours one way and Gage planned to be back in his tent at the McCormick Tract with eyes closed by 8:00 a.m. the following morning, at the latest. He pulled the small back pack to the front seat and pulled out a map from an outside pocket. The map outlined the streets of downtown Gaylord, and the directions to the Richards' home were highlighted in yellow.

Gage had not so much as cracked a smile since he found out the true reason for his brother's demise. All he could do now was drive, and he did so with a stone cold expression upon his face. He made sure not to exceed the speed limit, not even on the Seney Stretch because his alibi could be proven false if he were pulled over. Gage wore his cap low as he entered a gas station in Newberry, in the eastern Upper Peninsula. He paid for the gas with cash and then continued on towards the Mackinac Bridge, it was 10:45 p.m.

Gage wasn't nervous. Consequences were not contemplated. Everything that he intended to do was justified by the love for his brother. He went over the plan once again to make sure all was in order, and then prayed for all to go well. The items in the back pack consisted of a change in clothes, a zip lock bag with two envelopes inside, a pair of shoes, two pairs of rubber gloves, and a 45 caliber pistol. The pistol was purchased years before from a stranger through a classified ad in the Marquette Mining Journal, a newspaper circulated throughout the central UP. Gage bought it when he was sixteen years old and had not used it since. He found that he didn't care much for the pistol so it was stored below one of the bunks at the deer camp and had not been touched until the day before. The serial numbers had been scratched off by whoever owned it before him, and he had removed all fingerprints after taking a few practice shots days beforehand.

The town of Gaylord, Michigan was reached at 12:30 a.m. and Gage pulled onto Simmons Road after exiting from the highway.

The Richards' home was easy to find. Gage parked in an alley directly across from the small home owned by Brett and Frank Richards. He started to become un-nerved. He began to shake, as he finally considered what would happen to him if he were caught. He would be arrested and sent to prison, and his mother would not survive the loss of her second son. The children would have an even more difficult life without their Uncle Gage. And he would never marry Josie Strong.

Gage sat in the truck for twenty minutes, waging a mental battle with himself while staring into the dimly lighted home across the street. The fact of the matter, in Gage's view, was that Brett Richards would never be charged with the murder of Roy Gustafson. There was no evidence and no weapon, and a motive that was known only to Gage. The rage came back and he clenched his teeth. A pair of plastic gloves were put on and the loaded pistol and zip lock bags were extracted from his back pack. Gage walked across the street in darkness, hands in his pockets. The blue Ford Explorer was parked in the driveway and he snuck up beside it to look into the living room window. Inside there was a man in a recliner sleeping in front of a television. Without thinking anymore, Gage moved down the driveway further to try the door. It was open. He walked into the home quietly with the gun now at his side. Gage noticed that he was sweating profusely as he walked into the room where the man lay sleeping in the recliner. The room reeked of spoiled food, marijuana and body odor. The man's arm had a turnkit wrapped tightly around it and a syringe lay on the coffee table nearby. Gage raised the gun and realized that he could not turn back now.

"Wake up" Gage said loudly.

Brett Richard's bloodshot eyes opened and closed several times before he focused on Gage. When he noticed the gun, his mouth opened wide and his hands gripped the arms of the recliner tightly.

"Who the fuck are you man? Are you here to collect for

Abrams? Tell him that I'll have the money next week. Get that gun out of my face would you!"

"I'm not here for anybody" Gage replied. "Is there anyone else in this house?"

"No."

"Are you Brett Richards?"

"Yes. What the fuck do you want? Who are you?"

Brett Richards was fully awake and his voice trembled with fear. He started to stand up and Gage kicked his leg hard.

"Sit down and shut the hell up!"

"O.K." Brett mumbled sheepishly as he leaned back into the chair.

Gage Gustafson was not himself at that moment. He had transformed into a cold-blooded criminal on a mission to avenge his brother.

"I'm the brother of Roy Gustafson from the Upper Peninsula. Do you remember being at his camp on September 16th of last year? Before you answer, I'm going to say one more thing, it's very important. If you lie to me even once during this conversation I'm going to kill you. I will pull the trigger and shoot you through the eye. Now I'm going to ask you again, do you remember being at Roy Gustafson's camp on September 16th of last year?"

"I don't know what you are talking about" responded Brett.

Gage stood over him saying nothing for several seconds. It was obvious that Brett was very high on whatever it was that he shot into his arm with the syringe that lay nearby.

Gage moved. He moved quickly towards Brett with the gun extended and forced him to lean back hard into his chair. The muzzle of the pistol was now near the forehead of Brett Richards. Gage wanted to kill him; he badly wanted to kill him.

"Don't shoot me man. Please don't shoot!"

"Shut up you worthless bastard," Gage growled as he considered what to say next.

"If you tell me the truth you're going to live, but if you lie to me again it's over for you pal."

Gage moved the gun away from his head and backed up a few steps.

"Now listen up real close and don't say a fucking word until I'm through ok?"

"Alright" Brett said quietly and submissively.

"I know you were at the camp on that day in September, a good friend saw you there. My friend is in the military and left for Germany that same afternoon, so I didn't find this out until he called recently and it came up in a conversation. He saw the Ford Explorer with Florida license plates that you've got parked outside this house."

"You killed my brother. And now I'm going to kill you unless you do exactly as I say."

Gage stopped talking, hoping to hear an admission from Brett Richards. He held the gun steady, four feet away from his head.

"Please don't shoot me!" pleaded Richards.

"I......I really don't know what you're talking about."

"Then why the fuck were you at the camp?! You're a miserable liar."

Gage drew the hammer back and bore down, fully willing to pull the trigger.

"Wait! Wait a fucking minute! Alright, Alright man."

Richards was high and wreaked of bourbon. He was not in a state of mind that would allow any mental maneuverability.

"I was bombed man! I don't really even remember what happened. He wouldn't pay us. He owed us money. He had a gun and there was a struggle. The gun went off and he was dead."

Gage had all he could do to restrain himself from pulling the trigger. The tears were trying to leave his eyes but he refused to break down.

"Stand up and walk over to your kitchen table." Brett didn't move other than a continuous, steady shake.

"NOW!"

"O.K."

Richards got up and began to walk towards the table.

"Slowly" said Gage.

"Alright."

Richards sat down and Gage positioned himself at the opposite side of the table. He pulled the zip lock bag that held the envelopes out of his jacket pocket, along with two pieces of notebook paper. Brett looked puzzled as he tried to figure out what Gage was doing.

"You are going to write two notes, two identical notes that admit to the murder of my brother. One will be sent to my parents and the other will be sent to the Michigan State Police Post in Negaunee. You will also write the addresses on these envelopes and I will mail them. Do you understand me?"

Brett did not respond. Gage stood up from the opposite side of the table and moved towards Richards, seating himself one chair closer. He raised the gun once again.

"Please say you won't do it. Please tell me no so I can execute you as you did my brother" said Gage.

"Alright! I'll do it."

"Smart move asshole." Gage pushed the first piece of paper towards Richards, followed by a pen.

"Now you are going to write exactly what I direct you to, word for word."

Brett picked up the pen like an eager student, convinced that he would die if he refused.

"O.K. man, I'm ready."

Gage slid the two postage paid envelopes across the table followed by a piece of paper which included the names and addresses of his parents and the Michigan State Police Post in Negaunee.

"Copy the addresses on those two envelopes and make sure you include your address in the upper left corner."

Richards did as he was directed and slid the envelopes back to Gage. Gage then passed him two sheets of blank paper followed by another with a short, hand written letter stating that he was at the Gustafson deer camp on September 16, 1996, and that he murdered Roy Gustafson.

"Copy the letter twice, word for word" instructed Gage with an impatient tone.

Brett Richards hesitated. He looked at Gage and then to his left, apparently struggling to find the words to formulate a question.

"It's pretty simple scumbag, do it or fuckin' die."

I'd much rather you spend the rest of your life in prison, which is exactly what will happen to you if you write these letters, but be assured that killing you is my second best option."

Richards quickly started writing, copying the template letters word for word. He then pushed the letters back to Gage, and Gage inserted each of them into proper envelopes and put the template back into his pocket.

"One more thing, I want you to lick and seal the envelopes. I'll mail them today so you'd better start running. They will be coming for you soon."

Gage held the envelope to Brett's face with his left, gloved hand while holding the gun steady with his right.

"Why don't you lick them?" Brett asked.

"DNA is why Brett, you must think I'm stupid. Didn't you watch the OJ Simpson trial? Now lick the fucking envelopes."

"I didn't want to shoot him! I just wanted the money." Richards' yelped.

"Roy wouldn't listen to us and wouldn't pay the money, he began a struggle and the gun went off. It just went off man!"

The statement again created a picture in Gage's mind, a horrific picture of the very moment that his brother was killed. He began to lose what little self-control remained.

"Open your God Damn mouth and lick the envelope!" Gage yelled as he moved himself within two feet of Richards.

The first envelope was held to his face with the barrel of the gun inches behind it. The hammer was locked back once again. Richards immediately stuck his tongue out, now breathing heavily without any sense of rhythm. Gage brought the adhesive portion of the envelope to Brett's tongue and then sealed it before placing it in a plastic bag and his pocket.

"How could you kill such a wonderful man and father?" Gage asked quietly as he appeared to settle himself down, tears streaming from his eyes.

"You're not going to get away with this you know" said Brett.

"I was never here Brett. I have a solid alibi and your word will not stand up in court. A good friend of mine will testify that you were at the camp that day, and you will spend the rest of your miserable life in prison."

"We'll see about that. If they had any evidence they would have come for me long ago."

Brett Richards suddenly appeared to be somewhat relaxed, confident that he would still get away with murder. As the heroine continued to pump through his body he briefly considered an attempt to take the gun from Gage, but he was sure that death would follow if he failed.

The two men stared at one another during a very long moment of silence and hatred.

"Alright Brett, one more envelope and I'll be on my way." said Gage very calmly in an almost friendly tone.

"Fine" Richards said sarcastically as he opened his mouth slightly to extend his tongue.

And then Gage Gustafson forced himself to do what he thought was necessary... Brett Richards felt Gage's strong hand on the back of his neck and the cold steel barrel of the .45 caliber pistol powerfully forced into his mouth. Brett began to struggle fiercely, but only for a brief moment until Gage pulled the trigger. The discharge sent him reeling backwards over the chair and his body was lifeless only seconds later, after landing on the kitchen floor.

Gage was mortified. It was indeed the most gruesome sight he had ever witnessed. A portion of the wall behind where Richards sat was covered in blood and brain matter, and the murdered man was no longer recognizable. Gage became nauseous as he examined the lifeless body and quickly turned away. He stood there in the dark kitchen, temporarily paralyzed by what he had done, and then attempted to collect himself a few minutes later after the children entered his mind. Khora and Otto, who would now depend upon Gage to raise them and provide their primary source of happiness, needed Gage to make it home. He planned to raise them to become exemplary people, but he could not do that if he did not cover up the crime and return promptly to Upper Michigan.

The second envelope, of which Richards was about to lick when Gage executed him was placed back into a zip lock bag along with his gloves. Gage would dispose of these items later because of the blood splatter. He put a new pair of plastic gloves on and the gun was placed in the right hand of Brett Richards without allowing himself to view any other part of the dead body. Gage then peeked out of the window to see if all was still quiet outside. It seemed to be, so he carefully opened the door and walked briskly across the dark street to the mailbox. The letter addressed to the Michigan State Police was placed inside and the mailbox flag was propped upward.

The front seat of the Chevy extended cab truck had been covered by a sheet the night before to ensure that any blood on his clothes would not be deposited inside the truck. Gage could not see any blood on himself but he knew that it was likely that some was present on his clothes.

He vomited quietly outside before stepping into his truck, unable to shake the recent sight of a nearly headless dead man.

He drove away nervously at 1:30 a.m.

Chapter Twenty-Two

The drive back to the McCormick Tract seemed to last for eternity and his focus was interrupted often by bouts of uncontrollable sobbing. Gage abided by all speed limits once again and stopped only once to relieve himself at a vacant turnaround on the Seney Stretch. Feelings of nervousness, guilt and grief caused him to consider turning himself in. What he had done blatantly disregarded the most important Commandment. Gage prayed and then he wept again, and then he prayed some more.

He drove through Marquette and north on County Road 550 to County Road 510, and finally arrived at his original parking spot off of the Triple A at 6:45AM. He had not seen a single vehicle since passing through Marquette. Gage loaded the wrapped up sheet into his backpack with other incriminating evidence, turned on his flashlight, and walked briskly to his camp site on the Yellow Dog River. He arrived just before the day began to break and immediately started a fire. Totally worn out physically and more so mentally, Gage burned his backpack, clothes, shoes, cap, and all other evidence. He changed into clean clothes and continued to feed the fire with dry wood until all of the evidence had burned away. And then he crawled into his tent and fell quickly asleep. Gage dreamed about his brother and those beautiful children who were robbed of their father, and he dreamed about Frank and Brett Richards.

Despite the forty degree temperature of that morning in late

May, Gage woke up sweating profusely. His sleeping bag was wet. He felt worse now than before his long nap, not able to rationalize what he had done. He knew that if he could not justify murdering a murderer, his life would no longer be worthwhile. Gage would not be able to raise the children as his brother would have, nor would he be able to carry on with a successful career. And there was also the possibility of being caught. This in itself would haunt him for a very long time. Josie would not marry him if he confided in her. He would somehow have to put the murder behind him, somehow. Gage sat by the burnt out fire for awhile and then used a metal shovel to place all of the ashes in the Yellow Dog River, which swiftly carried away any remains of existing evidence.

At 10:00 a.m. he packed up, walked back to the truck, and drove home. Before he departed from the camp site, his wallet was placed under a hemlock tree near the river. This was another important step in his premeditated plan.

Even though Gage was gone for only one night the children were very excited to see him return. He hugged them as though he had been gone for an entire month while fighting back tears. At that moment, Gage realized that he must somehow cope with what he had done, he must be able to move forward. The children's love and the love of his parents and friends must provoke him to rise again. And then there was Josie. The woman he intended to marry would patiently see him through it, without ever knowing what he had done. The secret would never be shared with anyone; Gage would need to carry it to his grave. He could however confide in his dead brother, and planned to do so often in an attempt to free himself of guilt.

Gage spent most of the day with the children even though he continued to be exhausted, and then asked his parents to watch them for a few hours while he and Josie returned to the McCormick Tract to find his lost wallet. Gage spotted it under the hemlock tree near the river after ten minutes of searching. If the police questioned Gage about his whereabouts on the night of Brett Richards' death, his camping trip at the McCormick Tract would now be additionally supported by Josie. Gage was not taking any chances; he had meticulously pre-planned all aspects of his ghastly crime and cover-up.

Gage was in an agonized state of mind over the next few days as he anxiously waited to hear from Trooper Tornberg, hoping the letter would soon arrive. Perhaps someone heard the shot and snuck out into the dark street to write down his license plate number as he drove away afterward? Maybe the police found evidence that linked him to the crime and at any moment they would burst through his door to arrest him for murder? These possibilities were thought about relentlessly, without his control, and sent Gage to the brink of insanity. He could not eat much and slept very little on Friday and Saturday and kept the phone nearby at all times.

It finally happened on Sunday afternoon when his parents and Josie were over for brunch. The children were playing with friends in the yard, enthusiastically enjoying the long awaited spring temperatures while the adults watched from the porch. Sarah and Robert Gustafson were still heartbroken by the loss of their son Roy but their outlook had improved somewhat over the prior several months, albeit very slowly. Gage was sitting on the porch swing with one arm around his mother when the phone rang. He nonchalantly picked it up.

"Hello" said Gage.

"Hello Gage. This is Trooper Tornberg, can you come down to the post in Negaunee right away?"

The call he had been waiting for had finally come and yet Gage suddenly wished it hadn't. An extreme sense of nervousness began to overwhelm him as he stood up from the swing and walked out into the yard.

"What is it officer?"

"There's been a development in your brother's case. I would rather talk to you about it in person."

"What sort of development?"

"Can you come down Gage?"

"Ok, I'll be there in ten minutes."

Gage hung up the phone and explained to his parents and Josie that he needed to go.

"What's going on Gage?" his mother asked.

"I don't know mom, I'll call you when I get back."

Gage hugged his mother and Josie before he left. Robert Gustafson stood on the porch with a concerned expression on his face as Gage drove away.

Gage drove much more slowly than usual on the way to the State Police Post in Negaunee, praying one more time for God to forgive him and to allow his life to go on. He spoke to himself out loud on the way, emphasizing that he must not show any suspicious behavior. He had practiced for this moment dozens of times over the previous few days. Forcing himself to set aside the nervousness after rehearsing what he would say one last time, Gage parked the truck and asked his dead brother Roy for strength once again.

"Please Roy; please give me the strength to get through this brother."

Tornberg was standing behind the front desk when Gage walked in.

"Please come back to my office Gage."

Gage shook hands with the Trooper and followed him through a hall and into his office. The door was then closed.

"What's going on?" he asked.

"Please sit down Gage."

"O.K."

Gage sat down and Tornberg walked behind his desk and did the same.

"We received a letter yesterday from a man in Gaylord by the name of Brett Richards. Do you know of him?"

Gage shook his head slowly, carefully appearing not to be entirely certain one way or another.

"No, I don't think so. I know some Richards' from Ishpeming

but none that are named Brett. Why, what's this all about Trooper?"

"Gage, Brett Richards claims in his letter that he was at your camp on September 16th of last year, and that...and that he murdered your brother."

"Oh my God!" Gage responded loudly as he bent over with his hands over his face, slowly forcing himself to tear up by thinking of his brother. He had rehearsed the reaction at least a dozen times over the weekend. Trooper Tornberg stood up and walked over to Gage and then placed a hand on his shoulder.

"I'm so sorry Gage."

A few minutes passed as Gage collected himself and eventually made eye contact with Tornberg once again.

"Why?"

"We don't know. There's more Gage. After receiving the letter yesterday, I immediately called Trooper Kristen Swanson in Gaylord to inform her and to request assistance. She drove to Richards' home to arrest him, or to look for clues of his whereabouts if he was not at home. Mr. Richards did not answer the door so Trooper Swanson and two others entered the home with a warrant. They found Richards dead inside Gage."

Tornberg watched Gage and waited for a response. Seemingly shocked by what he had just been told, Gage sat back up in his chair and placed his hands on his cheeks, eyes swelled from tears that fled from his eyes.

"Dead?" Gage inquired.

Trooper Tornberg was a veteran of the Michigan State Police and had handled dozens of murder cases during his career. He would not rule out any possibilities until more facts were uncovered. Before transferring to his home town of Negaunee, Tornberg worked for years in Detroit and witnessed many bizarre criminal scenes. He observed Gage closely for any suspicious body language.

"Yes. Apparently he committed suicide just after he wrote the letter on or about last Thursday."

"The kids and my parents are going to be devastated all over again."

Gage did not address what the officer had said about the probable suicide of Brett Richards. His only noticeable concern was for his parents and for the children of Roy Gustafson.

"I should have known Roy would never have committed suicide."

"I'm so sorry Gage. There was absolutely no evidence of foul play surrounding your brother's death until now. We still need to find out what the relationship was between Roy and Mr. Richards. I've been working on it all morning and believe me Gage, I will discover what happened."

Gage waited patiently for the opportunity to drop a clue but didn't want to draw any attention to himself while doing so.

"The only information that I have right now is that Brett Richards and his brother Frank moved to Gaylord from Punta Gorda, Florida about a year ago. These were bad actors Gage, with a long history of criminal activities including drugs, attempted rape and theft. Both have been in jail numerous times. The brother Frank died from a drug overdose shortly after they moved to Gaylord."

Gage recognized an opportunity.

"Wait a minute, did you say they moved from Florida" said Gage softly.

"Yes."

"I'm not sure if this will help you or not, but Roy bought a large piece of land from two brothers that lived in Florida. They inherited it from someone locally, but I don't recall the name. What I do remember is that these two men from Florida showed up again after selling the property to Roy, asking for more money. My brother told me about it long ago and was very upset. They were alleging that he didn't pay them what the land was worth. Roy told me it was ridiculous that they demanded more money from him, and he nearly got into a fight with them when they showed up on the land while he was working there.

I have no idea if this is related or if these are the same people you are referring to, but it certainly is something that you should check into."

Tornberg returned to his chair, and sat down while a curious look overtook him.

"That's very interesting" he said.

"Did you meet either of these two men?"

"No I didn't."

"If the land was purchased from these criminals there will be a record of it, a deed recorded at the Marquette County Courthouse" Tornberg said.

"I'm sure my brother would have records of the sale in his office somewhere also."

"He would?" asked Tornberg. "Perhaps I'll drive over to his house to take a look in his office today, with your permission of course."

"Yes, please do."

"Thanks Gage, I will call you within the hour. It would be helpful if you could look through his records between now and then."

"I'm not sure where they are exactly but I'll be able to find them."

Gage got up from his chair and shook the Trooper's hand while nodding a thankful gesture, and began to walk out of the room.

"Gage, one more thing."

Gage stopped abruptly and turned around.

"You should probably hold off on breaking the news to your parents until we have absolutely confirmed this as a suicide. I know this is a lot to ask of you, but the coroner will be contacting me today or tomorrow morning after she examines the body."

"Alright, I'll keep it to myself until you hear from the coroner."

Gage drove to his brother's home and snuck downstairs to retrieve the folder titled "Fence Road Piece" from the office. He sat down feeling exhausted, satisfied and somewhat surprised with his recent performance, and waited for thirty minutes while thinking of fond memories of his brother. He left the house before anyone noticed and couldn't help but to drive back to Tornberg's office in Negaunee.

"Trooper Tornberg, my brother purchased the land from Frank and Brett Richards, all of the information is in this file."

Tornberg eagerly looked over the documents for several minutes.

"This information is very important Gage. We have now established a motive and I will confirm the sale of this property with the Marquette County Clerk tomorrow morning. Also, I just got off the phone with the coroner a few minutes ago. She has officially ruled suicide as the cause of Brett Richards' death. She explained to me that Mr. Richards was also using some heavy drugs just prior to his death."

Gage could not help but to express his anger, and this time his words appeared to be as sincere as ever.

"I wish that son of a bitch was still alive so he could spend the rest of his miserable life in prison."

"Me too Gage. You can tell your family now. A press release will be going out to all media outlets at some time tomorrow."

Gage stood up and embraced Trooper Tornberg before excusing himself, and while he did he began to cry, relieved that he would not go to jail.

Chapter Twenty-Three

Gage travelled home to explain the bittersweet news to his family and would do so on many occasions when asked by other relatives and friends. Over time the family and children began to heal and even Gage eventually forgave himself for his terrible sin, aided by the work of God.

Gage and Josie became married one year later and Josie was able to land a teaching job in their home town of Ishpeming. Together they gracefully raised Khora and Otto and added three more children in coming years. Gage never returned to Green Bay and took great pride in managing the financials of the Gustafson Land and Log Company. A forester was eventually hired to manage daily field operations and production, which allowed Gage to finally reach his dream of becoming a financial planner. Bart Collins, the financial planner that he had met with years prior, sold his business to Gage in the year 1999.

After raising five wonderful children, and capturing each and every career dream he held throughout his life, Gage Gustafson died near a trout stream at eighty-nine years of age. A blood clot took him quickly as he lay amongst tag alder and meadow rue near the sound of his favorite stream, and the last memory that passed him by was of his brother, Roy Gustafson. And they were reunited shortly after.

About The Author

Kevin Swanson is a life-long resident of Michigan's Upper Peninsula, and his most enjoyed hobbies include the pursuit of brook trout and ruffed grouse in remote areas seldom visited by others. Kevin is employed as a Wildlife Management Specialist with the Michigan Department of Natural Resources, Bear and Wolf Program. He resides in Ishpeming, Michigan with his loving wife and three children.

After experiencing the devastating impact of suicide first-hand through the loss of loved ones, Kevin began the journey of writing this novel in an effort to cope with those losses, and to raise awareness of depression as a serious mental illness. The manuscript was set aside for over a decade as fatherhood responsibilities consumed most of his free time. But finally, after being prompted by his family and friends, the manuscript was revisited and published.

Made in the USA
Lexington, KY
09 August 2017